https://www.brindlebooks.co.uk

CRIME WAVE
AT TANGENTS

BY

RODERICK EASDALE

Chapter 1

On seeing the sign for Tangents Golf Club, Marmaduke remarked to himself "mission accomplished", adding: "well the first stage anyway." He drove towards a handy-looking parking space then, seeing that it was reserved for the Captain, stopped his car, reversed and headed for another empty space. When he saw that this space was reserved for the Lady Captain, he retreated his car once more, this time to a more distant position well away from the clubhouse.

Walking towards the clubhouse, he was wished a cheery good morning by a well-upholstered middle-aged man of friendly countenance. He replied with an equally cheerful-sounding: "Good morning, fine morning is it not?" Then he wondered if the other's greeting was not as friendly as it had appeared; maybe it was more a polite code for 'explain yourself young man, what are you doing on our private golf club premises.' In case it was the latter, he added: "I am here to see Harry King. You don't happen to know where he may be found do you?"

The other gentlemen paused for a while, looking thoughtful and puzzled. "Harry? Don't think I know anyone... oh yes, of course, you mean Harry! Yes, of course, young writer chappie?"

"That sounds like him."

"Sorry, haven't seen him about today. You playing golf with him? It's a fine morning for it."

"No, he suggested I meet him here rather than at his home."

"Oh, I'd try the bar area first. Go through yonder door and, whenever given a choice of route options, favour the left option each time except when you should be going right and you'll end up in the bar."

"Thanks. Well enjoy your game," said Marmaduke, as a means of farewell.

"Young man, I am about to take some exercise with some most agreeable company, followed by what I have high hopes will be a splendid lunch. Anything else that might happen during the course of the morning I shall regard as a bonus. Ah Wilko!" he greeted someone coming round the corner. "Oh please excuse me," he said to Marmaduke. "Can I have a quick word with you, Wilko?"

"Yes, of course. Who was that chap? Not here to meet Rikki or Anun by any chance is he?"

"No, they are away at uni, Wilko, sharpening their intellects and studying hard."

"Is that what you did at university?"

"I'm sure I did. Some of the time anyway. Probably."

"I didn't much. I remember it as a wonderful time of going to parties and chasing girls. It's where I met Mrs Wilkinson."

"Your mother?"

"My wife. Well, future wife then. That rather curtailed my chasing after girls, unfortunately. What was it that you wished to ask me?"

"That honours board for the King Tangents – has your committee had a chance to discuss it yet?"

"Oh yes, we did so at our last meeting. We were all in favour of it."

"Capital, capital."

"But we didn't think the decision was ours to make; we thought it would rather be a matter for the Estates Committee. So you'd better apply to them for permission. Hope you get it, as it would be a good idea. Sorry, must dash as I am taking my wife to the market."

"Cheerio, hope you get a good price for her," said Willoughby affably. He carried on walking and bumped into Martin Cowmeadow, Chairman of the Competitions Committee. "Ah Martin, I've just had a word with Wilko about the honours board."

"Did we get the green light?"

"He reckons it's the Estates Committee that we need to approach. So I'll ask them. Oh, if you see Harry, tell him a chap who looks like a camel is looking for him."

But when Willoughby went down to the 1st tee he found Harry there chatting to the vicar. "Morning padre; and Harry – a chappie was looking for you, has he found you?"

"No."

"Sorry, forgot to ask his name."

Harry laughed: "It wouldn't matter if you had."

"Tush tut, young Larry. You are getting as bad as Rikki in these unfounded accusations. I am not that bad at people's names. She does fib so. Youngish chap with a face like a camel if that helps?"

"My cousin Marmaduke is meeting me here. He has come down to advise me on that barn conversion I was telling you about. He works in the building trade, in my uncle's building company. He does a lot of chippying and I need some carpentry assistance. I suggested that he met me here as many people seem to have difficulty finding Paddock's Farm."

"I directed him to the bar, so you may find him there," said Willoughby. "Right ho, padre, you all set? You can have honour."

Harry waited to see the vicar tee off. The vicar's drive was short but straight, as Harry had thought it would be. "Nice shot, vicar," he said. He then walked away, feeling Willoughby, with his more erratic play, may not wish a spectator for his opening shot. Walking up to the clubhouse, he was greeted by another member: "Hallo

Harry, chap with a face like a camel is looking for you apparently."

"Cheers, I'm just on my way to meet him."

When Harry met up with Marmaduke, he found him on the terrace. "Hallo, my spies had told me you'd be in the bar. But obviously I have been fed faulty intelligence."

"I was, but the scary countenance of the man behind the bar made me decide to leave. He had the air that I was something unpleasant he had trodden in."

"I wouldn't take it personally. That is the Steward's default attitude."

"I'd already had an encounter with an old buffer who told me off for wishing him a good game, telling me all he was doing was having some exercise with some splendid fellows before a dashed fine lunch."

"Ah, that will probably have been Willoughby. Fellow who looks as though he had been ordered in the large economy size?" Marmaduke nodded. "His attitude to golf," continued Harry, "has always stressed the companionship and the food rather than the competitiveness angle. He's actually a jolly good bloke when you get to know him – he was the one who welcomed me and made me feel at home when I first became a member. He's Rikki's godfather and how I got to know Rikki really."

"The love of your life?"

"Yes, quite possibly."

"Oh, so you have to behave around this Willoughby character? Oh, and you and her have to behave together in his presence if he is responsible for her moral welfare and good character."

"There is no danger of her ever misbehaving. And it seems to work the other way with them – she sees it as her god-daughterly duty to police his moral character. She absolutely adores him though. Her father died when she was very young – well, before she was born actually – so Willoughby has always done the in loco parentis bit for the male half of the equation."

"So you have to impress on the godfather that you are a sterling fellow of fine, upstanding character worthy of his god-daughter and not a shameless seducer of lonely, rich widows?"

"Lonely maybe; widow definitely; rich most definitely not, sadly; and seducer – nothing of the sort. I am the unpaid help around the smallholding, or rather one who does it in return for free board and lodging."

"So you haven't been scandalising the neighbourhood with your louche writerly ways?"

"No, I am as pure as the driven snow. Indeed, when it snowed and I went out, people kept walking into me unaware I was there. I still have some of the bruises. Mrs Winsor wanted me to move in to help her when the girls were away at uni as looking after the smallholding exhausts her now and, well, I was happy not to have to pay rent any more while I am trying to establish myself as a writer."

"Oh Harry, sorry to interrupt you two." They looked up: it was Cyril Ramsbotham. "There is someone here to see you," he said importantly. "He looks like a camel apparently."

"Oh thank you, Rambo."

"Not at all," said Rambo as he marched off almost as self-importantly.

"Do you need to be somewhere?" Marmaduke asked Harry.

"No, that's fine."

"Oh... it wasn't me he was referring to was he?"

"I think the message has got garbled on its way to Rambo," Harry replied tactfully. "Which reminds me, are you needing, or wanting, a drink after your journey?"

"Thus underlining my non-camel qualities?"

"Eh?"

"Camels can last a long time without either food or drink, a week or two without water; months without food. They use their humps as a sort of picnic hamper I believe. Surely an apprentice co-manager of a smallholding should know such basic facts about the animal kingdom?"

"We don't have that many camels on the farm. And my interest in farmyard animals, I have come to realise, is limited. I do my duty by them, but can't say they fascinate me. I am like Anun in that."

"What have nuns to do with it?"

"Oh, sorry – Anun as in Rikki's elder sister; short for Annunciata. Her attitude to the livestock is one I can relate to as she does her duty by them, but she has little emotional involvement. Whereas Rikki is really into it. Rikki is her mother's daughter. She loves all the animal kingdom, especially her pig. I have been sucking up to the pig, hoping it will put in a good word for me on her return. I gave him a football last week."

"Have you not discovered yet that pigs can't speak?"

"Oh yes – I have been reading up on pigs. That was in chapter one. But they are intelligent creatures and they remember people and have lots of little ways of showing whether they like you or not."

"So you and the pig are on the way to becoming best buddies to impress Rikki and make her fall in love with you?"

"Yes."

"So you are acting the role of the daughter to the mother of your object of your desires, while the daughter's own godfather is acting the role of her father, while all the time you are trying to seduce the pig as a way of making the daughter fall in love with you, though you are actually the daughter in this scenario, so you are trying to fall in love with yourself using a pig? What interesting lives you country folk live."

"Do you want that drink? Perhaps a cup of tea?"

"Something hot would not go amiss. But not tea: I drink gallons of that at work. Something different."

"Oh blast," said Harry, slapping his thigh to feel his pocket, "I forgot to pick up my card from my desk."

"Oh, not the old sorry-I-forgot-my-wallet trick?"

"No, I have remembered my wallet. It's my members' food and drink card that I have left behind. Members can now only buy food and drink using this card, not cash. It's a new system designed to improve efficiency apparently. But it has struck some here that it is more a way for Rambo – that was who was just here incidentally, he runs the House Committee – to reassert superiority over the Steward after the cheese-and-onion crisp ordering fiasco. That reminds me, I must collect the last of the crisps for Rik-pig. That will please Mrs Winsor as now she will get only actual money for her baked goods. That'll help the family cash flow."

"Was I supposed to follow all that?"

"Sorry, yes: there is a deal between the club and Mrs Winsor. She has the concession for baked items sold in the clubhouse. Part of her payment for this is in cheese-and-onion crisps, which the club has a surplus of after Rambo messed up the ordering. Him messing up the ordering meant the Steward was put in charge of that, which hurt Rambo's pride, so he has been plotting his revenge. The card system is that revenge – now everything is lodged in the computer system and reordered automatically, or something. The club has finally worked off its surplus of crisps, so today's load will be the last lot."

"What do you do with all the crisps?"

"Feed them to Rik-pig."

"Oh, your new best friend."

"That's the fellow. Well, he will never be my best friend. Nothing against him, but I confess I don't like him overly much – but don't quote me on that. But I want him to consider me his best friend, or second-best friend anyway."

"Especially when Rik-pig chats with Rikki."

"Precisely."

"How many people and other animals does he know?"

"Well, just me and Rikki I suppose."

"I think you've cracked the second-best friend then. Do I need a card to buy a drink?"

"No, non members can use cash; it's we members who can't. So I'll have to ask you to buy the drinks as I've left my card behind," he said, handing Marmaduke his wallet. "I will have a tea please."

Marmaduke went into the bar. "Please may I order some drinks," he said to the Steward.

"Yes, Sir."

"Please can I have a pot of tea for one. And what other hot drinks do you have?"

"We have a range of drinks. What particular drink would you like?"

"Um."

"Would you perhaps be wanting a cup of Bovril, Sir? That is a popular warm drink I understand with some people."

"Gosh it's ages since I've had Bovril. Yes, why not – okay, yes, a Bovril please."

"If you wish a Bovril, Sir, I regret you will have to go to the halfway hut which is situated by the 10th tee. We do not serve Bovril here. But the halfway hut is under different management."

"Oh, what about cocoa then? Or will I have to go to the halfway hut for that, too?"

"No, Sir, a trip to the halfway hut will not be necessary to get a cup of cocoa."

"Oh good."

"No, Sir, the halfway hut does not serve cocoa."

"Please could I order a cup of cocoa then."

"No, Sir."

"No?"

"Well yes, and no, I suppose you might say if you want me to be pedantic. Do you wish me to be pedantic? I am here to serve you in whatever way you wish."

"So can I have a cup of cocoa then?"

"No, Sir."

"Why not? You said I didn't have to go to the halfway hut for that."

"No, I said the halfway hut does not stock it. But nor do we stock it here. That is what I meant by yes and no, Sir. Yes in that you could order it here, but no in that we don't serve cocoa. So there would be no point in ordering cocoa, but I can't stop you ordering cocoa if you wish to. Do you wish to order a cup of cocoa, or perhaps a mug of cocoa?"

"What about hot chocolate? Do you happen to serve that here can you tell me? Actually serve it?"

"Yes, Sir."

"Oh good – well I will have a hot chocolate then please."

"I regret, Sir, that we do not serve hot chocolate."

"But you just said that you did."

"No, Sir, with respect, I did not. You asked me whether I could tell you whether hot chocolate was served in here. You did not ask me whether hot chocolate was served in here. I am sorry if I have confused you by answering your question, Sir."

"Okay, better make it a pot of tea for two then please."

"Sorry, Sir, may I ask you to make it clear exactly what you wish to have? Is that a pot of tea for one and a pot of tea for two? Or should I make that a pot of tea for three?"

"One pot of tea. To serve two people."

"Very good, Sir. I shall bring it out to you."

"Thanks, we are –"

"I know where you are, Sir," the Steward cut across him.

After he had paid, Marmaduke retreated to the terrace. "Cor that was an experience," he remarked to Harry.

"Duelling with the Steward is one of the sports here. Welcome to Tangents Golf Club. Oh, you didn't order a coffee did you?"

"No, why?"

"He loves it when someone unsuspecting does that."

"Ah Harry," Harry and Marmaduke looked up, it was the Chairman of Estates. "Oh I see you have found him. Oh yes, I see what he means. Quite extraordinary," and with that that the Chairman of Estates walked away.

"Do I really look like a camel?" Marmaduke asked Harry.

"Perhaps only from certain angles. Don't get the hump about it."

"I won't."

"Good – that'll only make you look even more like one."

"So, what is the local gossip then?"

"Hmm. Gossip? Well a regular topic of conversation recently has been the Local Plan. Hey, that's your line of work isn't it?"

"What is?"

"There are more homes to be built locally – that is what the Local Plan states – and Tangents has been earmarked for some of them."

"Whereabouts in Tangents?"

"That's the point, no-one knows yet. It has yet to be determined. Lots of rumours only. Some people are on edge that it will ruin the village, or their views, or the landscape, or the feel of the place, or just cos people don't like change generally. I suppose if you have got used to a set landscape, the route of your regular walk, and so on, you don't like your way of life being disturbed."

"Ways of lives often get disturbed precisely because there is no new building," said Marmaduke. "Villages are struggling all over and the way to cure this is through more housing, but villagers are almost invariably opposed to this. But often it is the only way you can get enough chimney pots and so enough people locally to support local services such as a village shop or a post office or the pub – or indeed a golf club."

"We don't have a pub or a shop here," said Harry. "All we have is the golf club, which I suppose also acts as the local pub."

"Did you used to? Have a pub and a shop I mean."

"There was a pub once upon a time. It got turned into flats, thus providing the extra homes to support the local service which was closed to provide these extra households."

"If you can extend or expand a village sympathetically, you can make it a living entity again, rather than somewhere people go to sleep and sit in armchairs and watch their televisions and occasionally take the dog out for a walk. We property developers are cast as the bad guys spoiling the countryside, but people don't see that aspect. So, where might this new housing end up then? What's the inside view?"

"I don't know. Haven't really followed the discussions, I confess. I seem to be spending most of my time on animal husbandry and trying to carve out some time to write. So 'property developer' is what you call yourself now is it?"

"Well, it's sort of what the family firm does. But no, I suppose I can't really say that is what I am. I am part of the builder's workforce, general odd jobs man, specialism: carpentry. On the subject of which, tell me what I am supposed to do, or we are doing to this here barn of yours."

"Well it will probably be easier to explain in situ when we get there. But we reckon with a bit of imagination and know-how it could be turned into semi-decent living accommodation. I am hoping you can supply the know-how. Oh, and possibly some of the imagination in places."

"Ah Harry, I have a message for you."

Harry looked up. "Oh, do you Brian?"

"Do I what?"

"Have a message, Brian."

"A message?" said the other vaguely. "I have just been speaking to um, the um, Secretary. Fellow's mad as a hatter. Madder even. He is even more crazy than the last bloke. Fellow's gone completely potty."

"Has he?"

"Who?"

"The Secretary – gone potty?"

"Oh you've noticed it, too. Well hard not to, I suppose. He has been talking to me, um, well, lecturing me. He says he wants me and my membership committee to make the membership younger. How on earth can you make someone younger? What does he want us to do – issue everyone with rejuvenation cream? Invent a time machine? You can't make people younger. People become older and there's not a darn thing you can do about it. Yet Pirbright seems to think we can do something about it. He's potty."

"I think perhaps, Brian, he was more intending to say that he wanted the average age of the membership to come down, rather than he wanted your committee to make individual members younger. I think he wants the golf club to enrol more younger members," said Harry.

"Do you? Oh. Well um if that is what he means why didn't he say so rather than blether on about making people younger as though he was some mad scientist. Wish people would say what they mean, if that is what he meant – do you um think that is what he meant?"

"Yes, he was asking me the other day if I had any young friends –"

"That's a bit personal, isn't it, asking someone if they have any friends. Fellow's lost all sense of decorum. Willoughby's right: fellow's a perisher. I am sure you have lots of friends; well, some anyway."

"No, he was asking if I knew any young people locally who I could persuade to join the golf club. He seems perpetually exercised about our membership numbers; he was saying how numbers are dropping as some of the older members are leaving."

"Well um if the older members are leaving, that is lowering the average age, so he is getting what he wants," pointed out Brian, "so why is he bothering me about it? Silly fool."

"Well I think it's more that he wants to increase the number of members while decreasing the average age," suggested Harry.

"Can't blame them really," said Brian. "This is not really a course suited to the, um, more elderly golfer. Too many narrow paths and steep inclines to allow golf carts, and um well it's quite a hike up hill and down dale for some of the older chaps here."

"There was an interesting article in Golf Fortnightly," said Harry, "about how they are developing golf in some territories. Some countries are trying to introduce golf, but what happens is that everyone wants to build the biggest and best course in the area, and no-one wants to build the rest of the infrastructure of the game, so it's really only appealing to tourists, ex pats and the like and not the much larger native market. There aren't the driving ranges, the cheap-and-cheerful par-3 courses for people to learn the game in a relaxed setting rather than plunging straight in. Take here, for example: we are the only club around, but how are we going to get people interested in the game except by pitching them in at the deep end by playing a full-length reasonably tricky course. It's too hard for some beginners, so it puts them off, and it irritates others when some hacker is ahead of them learning to play and taking millions of shots and holding up all the other golfers."

"Did you have any young friends who want to join, Harry?" asked Brian.

"No."

"What about Rik-pig, or is he too into football now?" suggested Marmaduke.

"Oh, shame," said Brian. Then spotting Marmaduke, Brian addressed him: "You're a young fellow. Sorry, we haven't met so I presume you're not a member here?"

"No, I'm not."

"Sorry, Brian, I should have introduced you two – this is Marmaduke, my cousin."

Pleased to meet you, er Marma is it?

"-duke, Marmaduke, Brian," said Marmaduke.

"Oh a duke. Um. Oh, yes, of course your cousin's a king. That makes sense. Pleased to meet you Sir. Do you golf?"

"Well only a little and very occasionally."

"Oh good, do you wish to join our club?"

"Sorry, I don't actually live near here. I am just visiting. I'm staying with Harry here."

"Who, sorry?"

"Harry here."

"Oh I don't think I know him. He can't be a member. Oh, well please try and persuade him to join, too, when you next see him."

"Who?"

"The chap you said you were staying with – Harry Here."

"Er, well, um…."

"He'll do his best," cut in Harry. "You said you had a message for me Brian?"

"Did I?"

"Yes."

"What was it?"

"I don't know. You didn't say."

"Was it about camels, by any chance?" remarked Marmaduke.

"Camels? Why would it be about camels?" asked Brian.

"It's just that Harry has been getting a lot of messages about camels recently."

"Has he? No, it was um, it was um. No, by Jove you're right – it was about camels! That's very clever of you! Yes, there is a camel looking for you, Harry."

"Oh, thank you."

"It's in the car park."

"In the car park?"

"Why, where else would you expect it to be?" asked Brian.

"Er, well could be anywhere. I was expecting it perhaps to be in the bar."

"No, it wouldn't fit in there and um what would it be doing in there?"

"Ordering a drink? No, that is not likely from what I've just learnt about camels."

"No, I don't think it can um drink," said Brian.

"They can, they just don't that often. They can though," said Harry.

"How?"

"Well, through their mouth I presume. How else?"

"Oh, that's ingenious. I had a, um, a sort of doll when I was um little which you used to sit on a potty and pour water into its mouth and um it used to wee in the potty. Does your camel do something like that?"

"My camel?" queried Harry.

"Looks like you are going to have camels on your smallholding," said Marmaduke.

"Oh it's not a real one," Brian explained to Marmaduke. "It's not a real one. That'd be very odd wouldn't it, if we had a real camel in our car park," he said, chuckling at the notion. "Oh, Harry, did you order it for Paddock's Farm and it's come here by mistake?"

"I think there has been some miscommunication. I think perhaps the message was that there was someone looking like a camel who was looking for me?"

"Is there?"

"Yes, but I have found him."

"Oh good. Was he the chap who brought the camel?"

"What camel?"

"The camel in the car park."

"But I thought you said it wasn't a camel in the car park," queried Harry.

"It isn't. Well, not a real live one obviously."

"It's a dead camel?"

"No, of course not – the camel you ordered. It's arrived and it's in the car park – that was the message I had for you. I remember now."

"Well, thank you very much, Brian, for passing on the message. We are just going to the car park," he added, as Brian began to amble away. "If you've finished your tea, Marmaduke, we might as well head over to Paddock's Farm. Your car in the club car park?"

"Yes."

"We'll drive over then if you'll give me a lift, as I walked over. That way I can direct you. It's dead near but has a concealed entrance lots of people miss."

As they walked into the car park they saw in front of them a large wooden camel. Brian was peering in its mouth.

Chapter 2

"Good grief," said Harry. Marmaduke just laughed.

"So how does it work then Harry?" asked Brian. "There doesn't seem to be a chute to pour water down, though there's a hole; well, more a slight gap. But it'd be difficult to pour water in there."

"Sorry?" said Harry.

"Pouring water in it so that it can go to the potty."

"No, Brian, this doesn't drink water. Well, I doubt it: after all, camels only drink once every week or two. It was that doll of yours that sat on a potty."

"Oh, yes. Not the camel."

"It's a fine looking beast isn't it?" said Marmaduke who had been inspecting it with a professional eye. "Nice workmanship, too. A tip for you: you can always tell whether something has been done properly by looking at the joinery – is it sturdy, has it been stapled or glued, and does any glue show on the outside? Good joints will never be stapled, and the glue should not show. This has been done well, and neither are there any gaps between the joints – these slot together beautifully. This a quality piece of carpentry," said Marmaduke running his hands along the camel approvingly.

"But what is it doing here?" asked Harry.

"That I cannot tell you," said Marmaduke. "But it's been sanded well – no rough spots when you run your hand over the surface, and it has been sealed and waterproofed, which suggests it has been designed for standing outside, and perhaps even for being viewed close up. Though, looking at it, the wood used is not of the highest order, so maybe it is not intended to have that long a life. Or maybe the carpenter has just worked off some of his lower grade stock on an unsuspecting client."

"Ah well, it's not our concern whatever it's doing here," said Harry. "No doubt someone knows and we'll find out in time. Here comes the Secretary, he'll probably know."

"What on earth is that doing here?" demanded the Secretary.

"That was just what we were wondering," replied Harry.

"We were just admiring Harry's camel," said Brian to the Secretary. "But it doesn't go to the loo, you know."

"What?" said the Secretary, puzzled by Brian's comment.

"No, that was my um doll."

"What, you're behind this Brian?"

"No, it's nothing to do with me. Harry ordered it."

"You are going to have to move it from there," said the Secretary, moving towards Harry, "we can't have it blocking off space in the car park like that, people have got to use the car park. What on earth were you thinking in getting it delivered here?"

"I didn't."

"No, you didn't think, did you. Blocking everyone's access like that."

"No, I didn't –" but what Harry was going to say was cut off by the Secretary saying "Oh heck," and rushing back to his office, as he had spotted that Rambo was arriving. The Secretary shouted over his shoulder: "Get it moved Harry. Soon as possible please."

"What's this doing here?" demanded Rambo.

"We don't know," said Harry. "But the Secretary seems to think it is our job to move it."

"Why?"

"We don't know that either."

"Where does he want you to move it to?"

"We don't know."

"You don't seem to know much," chided Rambo.

"Fortunately I don't need to know, unlike you."

"Why do I need to know?" challenged Rambo.

"As the club historian, you are going to have to write about this aren't you in your book. The Curious Case Of The Camel In The Daytime, or whatever you will call that chapter."

"I don't think anyone is going to be interested in a wooden camel appearing in the car park," scoffed Rambo. "But something interesting I can tell you about the car park is that I was looking at some of the old pictures again yesterday, pictures of the car park, well not necessarily of the car park you understand, but with the car park in them. One was a picture designed to show the clubhouse for instance, but the car park was in front of it, in front of the picture I mean, not the clubhouse. Well it was in front of the clubhouse, too, of course, as the car park was in the same position as it is now, but it was in the front of the picture I mean and something I noticed, though it was not easy to see it at first as the picture itself has yellowed a bit, but on looking at old pictures, the parking spaces used to be marked out in yellow paint rather than the white paint they are now, and I was trying to find out when the change had been made. Some of the old pictures suggest that the lines were not even there originally and when they were introduced they were painted white, though of course it is hard to say for sure because the early pictures were all in black and white but you have an idea from the shade of white, or the tone as it were, you could say, whether the lines in the pictures were white or yellow, or rather not the lines in the pictures as they are white of course as it's a black-and-white photograph but whether the lines that are being photographed were white or yellow at the time. It's quite interesting isn't it?"

"Rambo, do you mind giving us a hand to move this?" said Harry hurriedly. "Why don't we move it into the Lady

Captain's space? She never uses that and that will get it out of the way for everyone else."

But Harry's quick thinking could not spare them another Rambo Ramble, as he embarked on a long story, without obviously a middle or an end, or indeed much point or interest, about his method of cataloguing the old pictures of the golf club that he had. "You were probably wondering why I was telling you all this," said Rambo at the end to Marmaduke.

"Well, I was rather," confessed Marmaduke.

"Sorry chaps: must just go and see the Steward as I forgot to collect the crisps," said Harry, beetling off.

"Well you see," said Rambo to Marmaduke, "I have written a history of the golf club, and after I had finished that, my wife suggested I branch out and write a history of the area. I was reluctant at first because I felt that my doing that would be neglecting my wife which might be unfair after all the support she has given me. She has converted the shed at the bottom of the garden into a writing room for me. She says all the best writers have a set pattern of work, and so I must do the same. So she makes sure I am out of the house by 9 o'clock and do a 9 to 5 shift in my writing hut. She says that is how the best writers work, so I must too."

"She has been very supportive, you see. Another way she has been so supportive is that I used to come back to the house for lunch and we used to have some interesting conversations over lunch, but she feared that if I broke off from my work and talked to her I would I might lose my train of thought, so she now brings me my lunch on a tray. Well she doesn't bring it in to me any more – she used to bring it into the shed, er, my writing hut, and I'd have a nice chat with her. But she was still worried that us having a chat in that way would put me off – I told her not to be so silly, it wouldn't. But she was very concerned – so she just leaves the tray outside the door now. She doesn't bring it on the best tray, as she has to place it on the ground, but the second best tray; well perhaps the third, it depends how you, well 'one' I should say, views the blue one. I don't happen to like it that much, but my wife seems to like it more than me, we got it when we –"

"Well we better not keep you from your work," said Marmaduke, interrupting hurriedly. "Thanks for helping with moving the camel."

"I can tell you some more about these old photographs if you like."

"No I mustn't keep you from your writing; your wife is quite right that a regular work pattern is essential. Anyway, aren't you playing truant if you are supposed to put in a 9 to 5 shift?"

'Well yes, but I have important business at the golf club. I am the Chairman of the House Committee, the Chairman. I am also the Chairman, the Chairman, of the Heads of Committee, which is the most important committee of the club. So I am often called away, like today, from my writing work by my important duties at the club."

"Well I really mustn't keep you. Goodbye."

"It wouldn't matter if I was a minute or two late getting to my desk. I can tell you some other interesting things, if you like, about this car park."

"Sorry, I promised to help Harry with the crisps," said Marmaduke, "so I can't stop," he said, already heading off towards the clubhouse. As he had no real idea where to go to see Harry, as soon as he was sure that Rambo had left, he walked back towards his car, where he encountered Willoughby carrying his clubs to his own car.

"Oh hallo again," said Willoughby. "Good grief, you're not still trying to find Larry are you?"

"Er, Harry, no – I found him okay. I know better than to ask if you played well, but did you have an enjoyable time out on the course?"

"Thank you for not asking if I played well. I got roundly trounced by the vicar. But, in my defence, I had a disobedient golf ball which refused to do what I wanted it to. Sometimes you get one of those and there is not a darn thing you can do about it. But the company was indeed excellent, which is far more important."

"Oh hallo Willoughby," said the returning Harry. "Your game's finished early."

"Yes, not the full 18 holes this week as the vicar has a funeral. Still, it means I can put on the nosebag a little bit earlier. Can I invite you two young gentlemen to lunch as my guests? I am on a diet at home so I can only eat at the club."

"Is that how diets work?" queried Harry.

"It's how my diet works," replied Willoughby.

"Very kind of you Willoughby," Harry said, "but we have lunch awaiting us at Paddock's Farm."

"Ah you're in for a treat there," said Willoughby to Marmaduke. "Mrs Winsor is a fine cook. She believes in feeding people. She is a fine wife."

"Well she's a widow, Willoughby," Harry pointed out.

"Yes, such a waste, such a waste. Have you ever noticed how the wrong people are wives? Incidentally, any idea what the Lady Captain is up to? I know she doesn't drive, but is she travelling by camel now? And doesn't it have to be an actual camel rather than a wooden one? Mind you, the running costs must be cheaper for a wooden one – cuts down on the food and drink bill for starters. Or would you need to get a MOT and a road fund licence for a wooden camel which a real one wouldn't need?"

"A camel wouldn't cost much in food and drink – they only have a drink every fortnight and meal every three months apparently," said Harry.

"Do they? The poor souls. How terribly dull and grey life must be for them," then, on reflection, he added: "My wife should have married a camel. That is the kind of husband she would approve of. Well, disapprove of marginally less."

"We put it there," said Harry, "the Secretary asked us to move it."

"The Secretary ordered it for her? I wonder why. Mind you, he is an odd bloke, our Secretary. We seem to attract them: first Pike, now him. Ah well, I mustn't keep you from your lunch; or you me from mine. Bon appetite chaps!"

"You too, Willoughby," said Harry.

Willoughby had been a keen reader and a lover of literature since his youngest days. His reading tastes ranged far and wide, encompassing anything from the classics of literature, the Complete Works of Shakespeare volume which he had proudly won as a school prize, to even the most trashy of detective fiction, or the short stories of Sherlock Holmes which he had enjoyed reading with Rikki when she was young. But, above all, the reading matter that was his particular favourite, and which gave him the most pleasure and which he looked forward to the most, was a well-constructed menu.

The Steward knew that when he handed Willoughby a menu it would not be a cursory glance and the quick decision made by some who came into the clubhouse; he knew that Willoughby would take his time, savouring and contemplating every line of it. The Steward knew better than to ask if he was ready to order yet, for Willoughby would tell him when he was; indeed, lost in contemplation of a menu, Willoughby would often be oblivious of anything going on around him, or of anyone speaking to him. The Steward was aware that he would be summoned when Willoughby had made his decision and there was no point in interrupting the process.

"Ah Steward, I am ready to order if you're ready," Willoughby said in due course.

"I am, Sir. I forgot to mention that, as a member, you will not be able to order anything unless you have your food and drink card."

"Fear not oh good and faithful servant, I have collected same from the office," said Willoughby waving it at the Steward. "I think I'll have the Scotch broth soup of the day please for a starter."

"Soup and roll, very good Sir," said the Steward writing it down on his pad.

"And for the main course, steak and kidney pie please and as I see that comes with creamy mashed potatoes and roasted carrots, I think a side dish of sautéed green beans would be perfect to provide a fresh, crisp contrast, and perhaps a few roasted parsnips would be fun, and I think the cauliflower cheese as the third side dish please."

"The cauliflower cheese is not actually a side dish, Sir. It is a main course."

"A main course just of cauli cheese?"

"It is what I believe is termed a light lunch."

"Light lunch? What an abominable idea. So I can't have the cauliflower cheese?"

"You can, Sir, but it will come as a main portion not as a side portion."

"That's okay, bung it into the order nevertheless. Ah, that

will unbalance things won't it? Lots of cauli cheese compared with the rest of the vegetables."

"It might perhaps be considered to do so, Sir."

"Okay, better order another lot of side dishes of green beans and parsnips then to balance it out."

"Very good, Sir."

"Oh, hang on, that does leave the vegetables rather dominating things."

"You do appear to have ordered what some may term an ample sufficiency of vegetables, Sir."

"Yes, it has become unbalanced again, so I'd better order another steak and kidney pie. That solves that. Then rhubarb crumble and custard for pudding please."

"So, Sir, that is soup and a roll as a starter; then three main courses, two of steak and kidney pie and one of cauliflower cheese; and four side dishes, two of green beans and two of parsnips. But just the one dessert, of rhubarb crumble and custard. Do you wish anything to drink?"

"Well, I could have a nice full-blooded red to complement that, maybe a Bordeaux or... no, better not include a glass of wine with the meal. I am on a diet."

"Very good, Sir." Shortly the Steward was back: "I am sorry Sir, but your order has been rejected."

"Oh dear, run out of one of the vegetables or something, have you?"

"No, Sir."

"What bit is the problem?"

"All of it, Sir."

"All of it!"

"Yes, Sir."

"What do you mean all of it?"

"You are unable to order any food."

"I can't order any food?"

"Yes, Sir, that is exactly the meaning I was hoping to convey by the use of those words."

"Why not?"

"Your card does not allow you to purchase food."

"My card – my food and drink card?"

"Yes, Sir."

"I can't buy food on my food and drink card? Does not the name of the card suggest this is a fallacy?"

"I had already noted that there was what might be termed a certain irony in the nomenclature of the card in question in this case, Sir."

"Why cannot I?"

"The card has been set up to only allow you to order drinks on it."

"Oh, I see, teething troubles on its first day of operation. Well bung the card through again and see if it plays ball this time."

"No, you do not understand, Sir – your specific card has been set up to only allow you to buy drinks on it, not food. It is a feature of this new system that these cards can protect people against ordering things they should not – for example, a person with a nut allergy can be protected against accidentally ordering something with nuts in it or the vegan from ordering something which is not vegan; those under age can be prevented from buying alcoholic drinks, and so on."

"But I am not an under-age vegan allergic to nuts."

"No, Sir."

"And from what you tell me, if it's correct –"

"I would hardly lie to you Sir."

"And I am sure that you would not, it is refusing me all foodstuffs not just nutty alcoholic vegan stuff. What does it think I am, a breatharian?"

"A breatharian, Sir?"

"Yes, those idiots who think they can survive on air alone and so don't eat food."

"Oh, I have never met one of those."

"Few people have – breatharians don't live long enough to be met by many people. Well can you re-set my card so that I can be allowed food?"

"I cannot. I have not the ways or means of doing so."

"Hang on – it will allow me to drink?"

"Yes, would you like a drink?"

"Soup is drunk so why won't it allow me the soup?"

"That is a question Sir, to which there are various possible answers."

"Well slosh through an order on that card system just for the soup then."

"I will endeavour to do that Sir." The Steward was back shortly later to say, "I regret that order has been declined."

"Why?"

"Various potential reasons suggest themselves."

When he realised that the Steward had finished speaking, Willoughby prompted him: "Which are?"

"One possible solution could be that those setting up the card are not as well versed in the finer points of the English language as you and me. Another is that we don't actually serve soup here."

"What do you mean you don't serve soup! It is on the board there – soup of the day: Scotch broth."

"Yes, Sir, that is the soup of the day, but we do not serve it."

"What do you mean you do not serve it. You do."

"We don't."

"Yes you do, it's on the menu."

"With respect, Sir, you are mistaken."

"Here get me a menu," commanded Willoughby. After

the Steward had passed him a menu, Willoughby jabbed angrily at it: "See there that line which says soup of the day under appetisers?"

"With respect, Sir, it says soup of the day with a bread roll."

"What's the difference?"

"Well, Sir, you cannot drink a bread roll."

"I don't want to drink a bread roll!"

"No, Sir."

"Oh, you think that maybe your stupid card system is refusing to serve me soup –"

"It is not my card system, Sir."

"Okay, the stupid card system then. That is why the card system is refusing to allow me to drink some soup?"

"I would not like to venture a definite opinion as I do not have the data, but that is indeed one of the possibilities."

"Okay, so let's order some soup without the bread roll then and see if the wretched card will deign to allow that."

"You can't order soup without a roll. We don't serve soup without a bread roll."

"Of course you can serve soup without a bread roll – just don't include a bread roll. Just bring out the bowl of soup."

"We can't do that, Sir."

"Of course you can. Just don't include the bread roll. Give it to the birds, knock it onto the floor and leave it there, don't take it out of the bread bin, feed it to the camel outside – there are endless possibilities. I don't care how you do it, just bring me the soup."

"The camel outside?"

"Yes."

"What is a camel doing outside?"

"At the moment, having as much food as I am."

"I see where you've got confused. You believe we can serve you soup but without a bread roll."

"Spot on."

"Of course we can bring your soup and not bring you a bread roll with it."

"Excellent – well do that then please."

"But we cannot serve food which has not been ordered."

"Well can I order soup without a bread roll?"

"No, Sir. But you can order anything to drink that you would like."

"I'd like to order some soup to drink then."

"I can bring you anything you would like to drink, apart from soup."

"Why on earth did you introduce this infernal system!"

"I did not, Sir."

"But I thought you were dictator here?"

"It appears that I am not."

"We never used to have it."

"No, Sir."

"So why do we have it now?"

"It was introduced, so I was told, to improve the ordering system."

"It doesn't seem to be achieving that does it?"

"That indeed may be one interpretation based upon the facts."

"So why do you not you just scrap it? Right now would be as good a time as any."

"It was not me who introduced it. It was the Chairman of the House Committee."

"Rambo! That boil, that plague sore who has not so much brain as ear-wax, that trunk of humours, that swollen parcel of dropsies, that huge bombard of sack, that prattling gabbler, wretched worm-filled good-for-nothing nincompoop, that loathsome wretch, that demented doddypolled mephitic maggot, that moronic mumpsimus, that stuffed cloak-bag of guts, that deranged dunderhead, that trandled strendelbarn, that watboddled dumpelrump, that blethering buffon, that blundering bobolyne, that cap of all the fools, a vanity in years?"

"I believe we are speaking of the same gentleman, yes Sir."

"And you are now claiming you have neither eyes to see nor tongue to speak in this place but as this House Chairman is pleased to direct you?"

"I would not have put it so poetically, Sir, but I believe your statement covers the essence of the situation. May I make a suggestion?"

"Go ahead," said Willoughby, slumped in the chair, his face a picture of misery.

"The food and drink cards were set up in the office, so perhaps if you go there you may find a solution to your particular problem."

"I am not going to find one here am I?"

"No, Sir." Willoughby got up and stomped off to the office in a bad mood.

The Steward returned to behind his counter in a good mood. He had far too much respect for the dignity of his position to hum a gay little tune, or even to let the barest flicker of a smile play across his face, otherwise he may have done so. But behind that stern facade he presented to the world when on duty, he was joyous. He was confident that Willoughby would not find out that it would have been perfectly possible to order just soup on its own; it was simply that the Steward had thought it might be more entertaining if he pretended that it was not. And so it had proved. The Steward had been gorgeously entertained and had enjoyed the recent exchange enormously.

The Steward also knew that if he got Willoughby implacably opposed to the new card system it could only help the Steward's own efforts to get the system jettisoned. The Steward enjoyed exercising whatever petty powers he could obtain and jealously guarded them, and he was wary of this new card system as that seemed to threaten that.

Meanwhile Willoughby, billowing like a galleon under full sail, crested the steps of the office and knocked and sailed on in. Miss Murtle looked up at the intrusion: "Oh good afternoon, Willoughby, what can I do for you?"

"Gosh, what a lovely dress that is," said Willoughby, stopping in his tracks.

"Oh do you think so, it's new. I was a bit worried the colours might be a little too bold."

"Bold they most certainly are, but you carry it off so delightfully, as always," replied Willoughby. "Is the Secretary in?"

"No, he has had to go out – an emergency meeting with the club solicitor, as a problem has arisen with the rent. Can I help instead?"

"I want some lunch."

"Oh dear, you have come to the wrong place. We are the office; you need the dining area," Miss Murtle tittered. "Sorry I should not tease you," she said, realising that Willoughby was not laughing with her. "Oh, you need to collect your food and drink card do you? Yes, you can't get fed or have a drink without it now. Load of stuff and nonsense strikes me as."

"Stuff and nonsense it is indeed. You could not have put it better," agreed Willoughby. "No, I have my card; collected it from Secretary fella this morning. But it doesn't work – darn thing won't let me order food on it."

"Oh dear, have you spoken to the Steward? What did he say?"

"He suggested that I come here."

"Okay, well let's look at the paperwork you filled in, perhaps there is a problem with that."

"Paperwork? I haven't filled in any paperwork. I just came in and collected a card."

"You must have filled in the paperwork to have had a card ordered. Huge long form it was. Lots of administration this flipping card system has involved. Right pain in the neck it has been."

"Oh yes, I remember a form arriving, but I just ignored it."

"Here we are," said Miss Murtle who had been going through the file. "Oh, I see your form was filled in by your wife."

"My wife? Oh she likes forms. But she obviously hasn't done this one very attentively. That's most unlike her, she's normally so good with them. Ah well, where do I need to sign to change that, so I can get some lunch?"

"Sorry, only the person who signed the form can make changes to it."

"Eh?"

"Yes, some people have a third party in charge of their cards, such as their parent, guardian, counsellor or sponsor. For example, children can have cards, but in their case a parent would fill in the card saying what they can and can't have, such as no alcohol, or no wheat products if the child has a wheat allergy. Or someone who is in AA might have a sponsor fill the card in to say that the card cannot be used to buy alcohol, that sort of thing."

"But I am not a child, or an alcoholic. Being married to Mrs C might cause people to think I had been driven to drink, and indeed a lesser man probably would have been, but I have remained strong."

"I understand that the idea behind this," explained Miss Murtle, "is that, say an alcoholic has a relapse and tried to buy alcohol the card protects him or her from doing so, as they cannot change the terms of the card – only their sponsor can."

"You mean, only my wife can change it?"

"Yes."

"My card," he added, stressing the first word.

"Yes, that's okay, isn't it," Miss Murtle said gaily, "tell her she has made a mistake in the paperwork and she can pop in and get it changed. Oh dear, but probably not in time for you to get lunch today."

"No, it was no mistake by her. I am on a diet, you see. This is her way of making me stick to it."

Miss Murtle looked at the picture of dejection in front of her and felt stirring pangs of sympathy. She was fond of Willoughby and it pained her to see someone normally so ebullient and always pleased to see her – he had noticed and praised her new dress, she was so pleased – utterly miserable. "I don't know what to suggest. There is nothing I can do. Perhaps if you spoke to Mr Ramsbotham as it was him who has introduced this system. But if you ask me, this silly system is not about protecting people with nut allergies, but of him reasserting dominance over the Steward. I think he is upset that the Steward was given sole control over ordering after that crisp business."

"How does this help?"

"The card system automatically tracks what everyone has bought and reorders it. It's Mr Ramsbotham's way of excluding the Steward from the process, it strikes me."

"Why is our perpetually hard-up club lashing out on this imbecilic system?"

"We are not. We have got it for free as we are conducting a beta test for the company behind it."

"What is a beta test?"

"I didn't know either, but apparently after something has been designed it is put through its paces to see how it works in practice before the product is sold commercially, to see if it works as intended, or if there are any bugs in the system that need ironing out. We are conducting the beta test on behalf of the company, so that we have been given it to use for free."

"So it's Rambo's wounded pride that has inflicted this system on us. 'Tis indeed pride that pulls the country down. Right, I suppose I'd better go and see that huge bombard of sack, that pestilent pumpkin-head, that watboddled dumpelrump, that motley-minded mangy moldwarp, that crusty batch of nature. Oh dear," and, with that, Willoughby stomped out in the highest of dudgeons.

Chapter 3

As Miss Murtle was returning from her lunch she spied, across the car park, Willoughby returning to his car. "Did you manage to sort out your lunch?" she called out.

"Well, sort of," replied Willoughby.

Miss Murtle entered the office and saw that the Secretary had returned. "Hallo, was it a good meeting with the solicitor?" she greeted him.

"Yes and no. Useful anyway. He confirmed that Benton Snivelgate has the law on his side and there isn't much that we can do about it. Curses."

"Oh dear. What an awful man Benton is."

"I've just bumped into him actually. He had been playing golf. On his own."

"Did you mention you'd just seen the solicitor?"

"Certainly not," the Secretary snorted. "I played the straightest of bats and didn't say anything about it. He was asking about that wooden camel in the car park."

"I was wondering about that. What is it and why is it there?"

"Harry King's doing. No idea why he had it delivered here. I've told him to move it. Apparently Harry has a friend coming to stay with him who is a carpenter, so Benton said. So presumably this carpenter has made it for Harry? But goodness knows why the carpenter delivered it here. But that is the least of my problems today. Anything happen when I was away?"

"No, just a few more people collecting their food and drink cards. Oh yes, and Willoughby was in here wanting a word with you."

"Oh glad I missed him, that's at least one good thing which has happened on this dark day. Sorry to have landed you with him, but then you seem to handle him better than I can.”

“Yes, my feminine charms do seem to have quite an effect on him don’t they?”

“Do they? Gosh, well, um, as I said you seem to handle him better than I can.”

“I don’t understand why you have a problem with him. I have always found him most kind and helpful to those he knows and likes.”

“I’ve always found him a pain in the posterior.”

“Oh. Shame.”

“What did he want? Whatever it is, I hope you said no? Shame Mrs Cornwallis doesn’t keep her husband locked in her shed, like Mrs Ramsbotham does; though it is a pity she lets him escape so often. She should be more vigilant. But I suppose Willoughby would find a way to escape, too.”

“Mrs Cornwallis might be more successful. She did after all spend many years in a prison.”

“Really?” said the Secretary, shocked. “What was she in for?” Then, a happy thought having occurred to him: “It wasn’t for killing a previous husband was it?”

“Oh, no, no. Nothing like that. She used to work there. She dealt face-to-face with some real hard cases: homicidal maniacs, the real thugs, that sort of thing.”

“That must have been scary.”

“Positively petrifying I imagine. But then they had committed serious crimes and were there to be punished so you can’t feel that sorry for them.”

“No, for Mrs Cornwallis I meant.”

“Oh for her? Oh. No, I doubt it.”

“I had not met her before, but when she came in to set up Willoughby’s card account she struck me, well, as, shall we say, a woman of determined character.”

"I think the phrase you are looking for is old boot."

"I could never use such a term, Miss Murtle, about a member's wife. It would be most unprofessional. But does the old boot give him a good kicking? Does she give him a hard time?"

"Willoughby thinks so."

"Oh. Shame."

"What did Willoughby want?"

"He wasn't able to have lunch."

"Is that our fault?"

"It turned out that he didn't know his card had been set up by his wife to exclude food so as to make Willoughby stick to his diet."

"Was Willoughby upset to find that out?"

"He did seem rather dejected."

"Oh. Shame," said the Secretary happily.

"Be a wee dent in the club's income if Willoughby won't be eating here any more. He must spend a fair bit."

"Every silver lining has a cloud," replied the Secretary.

While this conversation had been going on, Willoughby was in the car park talking to Brian. He had just been about to get in his car and drive home when Brian had come up to him and said: "I've just heard the news. Terrible isn't it?"

"Thank you. Yes."

"I was phoned and told the news."

"Good grief, were you? Who phoned you? The Steward?"

"No – the Greens Chairman."

"I thought all we had was the House Committee for catering? Though I know we had a wine sub-committee at one stage. We have a greens sub-committee, too, do we now? I suppose it's all this food miles business. Cor, this club doesn't half like creating committees. We'll have a committee for creating committees next."

"No, um, we've always had um a greens committee. I was on it briefly years ago," said Brian. "Or was it another committee I was on?"

"I've never been aware of it."

"You here for the unofficial um council of war in the clubhouse?"

"I wasn't aware there was one."

"Oh. Well you'd better come along. This affects you, too."

"Too darn right! Odd the promptness. It only started today. Seems unlike this club, such speed. Must have annoyed a lot of people."

"It has. Yes, Jerry said it only came to light today, but they need to act as soon as possible, so he suggested anyone who was around meet up and plan what to do. It's terrible isn't it."

"Yes, I couldn't have my lunch."

"It put you off your food? I can um understand that."

"No I couldn't order any food, that's the whole point. News travels fast here I know, but it seems a bit dynamic for this club for people to be acting so rapidly. But delighted it looks like being nipped in the bud. Silly idea altogether."

"Well I think it's partly panic really. We've only got a few days to decide what to do."

"Well it's simple surely – just scrap the whole damn silly thing. There's no point to it."

"Scrap the golf club?" said Brian, shocked.

"No, just the cards, Brian."

"We'd have to do more than that, but um yes, I suppose we'd have to get the cards changed if we're going to go down to sixteen," said Brian, "I hadn't thought of that."

"Sixteen cards! One is bad enough. What fresh insanity is this being proposed? Yes, I definitely think I'd better go in with you!"

Inside the clubhouse they were greeted by Jerry Best. "Hallo Jerry, what are you doing here?" asked Willoughby.

"Well I'm on Greens these days and the Secretary told me the news this morning."

"Absolutely no need to change things. The old way worked perfectly well," said Willoughby firmly. "No idea what he was thinking about. The old ways are the best, as Martin Cowmeadow keeps reminding us."

"Well what Benton is doing is fairly underhand, but we could have anticipated that perhaps."

"Well he is indeed the rankest compound of villainous smell that ever offended nostril. But what's he got to do with it?"

"Oh, I'll explain when everyone is here. Glad you could come, Willoughby: when I phoned your home your wife said you were out playing golf all day with the vicar. Sorry, did I interrupt your game?"

The Chairman of Estates arrived: "Just heard the news, dirty work afoot. But what can you expect from that louse."

"Careful," counselled Willoughby, "he might hear you, he's only over there."

"Where? No, he's not."

"The Steward, he's right there," said Willoughby pointing with his eyes.

"It's not the Steward's doing, you fool."

"No, quite; it's Rambo's."

"Rambo's? No Benton's you fool."

"Benton. Oh is he behind the cards – one of his dodgy schemes, I didn't know that. What on earth has the club got involved with him for? Asking for trouble. Oh yes, I meant to ask you about getting an honours board up for the King Tangents competition. Is it you I need to ask about that as Chairman of Estates?"

"Honours board? No, that's not us, surely wouldn't that be –" whatever else he might have been about to say was cut off by Jerry saying loudly "Okay," to the group milling about the committee room, "please do take seats those who haven't. I think that's everyone? Apologies for the short notice, but I thought it easiest if I got everyone together, or as many of the committee as I could, to explain what is going on and discuss where we go from here. I am not sure how many of you know, but the land for the 10th and 11th holes, and for the halfway hut also, is owned by Benton Snivelgate and leased to the club by him."

"The halfway hut doesn't use this silly card system does it? It's under separate management," pointed out Willoughby.

Jerry ignored this comment and continued: "The lease runs out in just over a year. He sent a letter about it when Pike was still Secretary and well, it seems to have been ignored as, well Pike was by then um not very well."

"Gone completely bonkers you mean," harrumphed the Chairman of Estates.

"Not functioning to his maximum intellectual capacity," said Jerry tactfully. "The letter appears to have arrived shortly before he was admitted to the sanatorium. Anyway the upshot is that we have only 29 days left now to tell Benton whether we wish to lease the land again in a year's time for a period of another 10 years or not. But the kicker is the lease is being increased tenfold in price and, frankly, not only is that a rip off but there is also a matter of how easily we can afford that savagely increased outlay."

"Can't we negotiate it down?" suggested someone.

"Benton is insistent he won't budge in price. Under the terms of the original lease agreement, he has found a loophole which allows him to do this to the rental fee and the club's lawyer told the Secretary this morning that there is nothing we can do about it. We either say yes or no. Benton has the law on his side."

"The law is an ass," snorted the Chairman of Estates.

"So we have no option other than to say yes and pay up?" asked someone.

"That may be so," replied Jerry. "But it sticks in the craw paying that devious crook a rip-off price for the two dullest holes on the course."

"Yes, worst holes we have," said another.

"Can't we call Benton's bluff?"

"What bluff?"

"Well what's he going to do with two golf holes if we don't rent them off him?"

"Build houses on them no doubt," replied Jerry. "The Local Plan dictates that we are to have more housing here. Benton presents this land to a developer and voila! He's probably hoping we don't renew our lease, as this gives him an out to make more money from that land. At present we have first refusal on that land."

"Would Benton get planning permission?"

"Almost certainly," chimed in another person, "and I imagine Benton is working on that belief, too. The Local Plan requires new houses to be built, so it will happen. Even if a way is found locally to turn it down, he can appeal to the Secretary of State and he can get it that way. Golf courses all over are being built over."

"Can we even afford to pay this huge rent?"

"I suspect not easily, well not at the moment," replied Jerry. "That's why I hoped the Chairman of Fundraising may have been able to make it. Oh, sorry, but we do have the Chairman of Finance," said Jerry holding out his hand as an invitation for the latter to speak.

"It will be a squeeze," said the Chairman of Finance, "and frankly do we want to squeeze the club for those two fairly mediocre holes? Risk going bust to keep open the two worst holes on the course and pay a truly foul man an exorbitant fee for doing so?"

"Well otherwise we end up with a 16-hole course," pointed out someone.

"Is that necessarily so very bad?" countered another.

"Well it'd be daft, how would handicaps work, or the club competitions? Be okay for social golf, but the rest of it?" said Martin Cowmeadow.

"Well one idea was that we drop down to a nine-hole course," said Jerry.

"What, lose seven more holes as well! That'd be terrible."

"Well nine holes is at least a recognised course length, unlike 16," pointed out Jerry.

"Is that what you suggest we do, Jerry?" asked someone.

"No, I was just throwing it open to the floor as it were. We appear to have various options, none of them that appealing, and that is perhaps one of them."

"That one is definitely unappealing," said Wilko.

"Well as I see it," said Jerry "and sorry to take the lead on this, but it's just that I have had longer to think about it than most here, as I was told about it earlier today, but the options which seem to be floating around so far are: one, that we pay Benton, but that may mean the club risks going bust down the line; two, we find the money from a rich benefactor, sponsorship, a big fundraiser, or whatever, bearing in mind we have so little time before we either say no or commit ourselves to 10 years' worth of rental payments; three, go to having a 16-hole course –"

"Whoever the heck heard of a 16-hole course," scoffed the Chairman of Estates. "That's ridiculous."

"Or four," Jerry continued, "in light of that, we go down to being a nine holer."

"That'd be sad," said someone.

Willoughby suggested: "I think it would be a good idea if we all discussed these options perhaps over scones and a pot of tea?" No-one reacted to his suggestion.

"Or can we," said someone, "get two more holes out of our existing land?"

"We thought about that, but we are fairly constrained already," said Jerry, "and the only really obvious way would be to divide two of the long holes into two par 3s each. But that will make the course much worse, especially as the two holes most ripe to be halved in length are two of our better holes, and we would end up with a rather diddy course: lots of par 3s and short par 4s."

"Yes that would make it a flipping mediocre design," said Martin to general murmurs of agreement.

"Sorry not to have anything concrete to suggest. It's all blown up this morning and caught me unawares," said Jerry. "It's not really a Greens Committee matter but one for the Heads of Committee, but I thought it best to put everyone in the picture at the earliest opportunity, and to encourage everyone to put their thinking caps on."

"I have an idea," said Willoughby. "Wouldn't it be better to sit down and discuss it over tea and scones, in a more relaxed, calm, reflective environment everyone?"

"Sorry, I have got to be off soon," said Jerry to Willoughby. "So have I," chimed in Martin.

"Why don't we find some land elsewhere and build two new holes on that?" suggested Brian.

"But where?"

"Winnie's Place has been up for sale for a while now with no takers," pointed out Brian, "and that has um a fairly extensive plot which abuts the course. Maybe we could get that cheap?"

"What, give up Benton's land and build two holes there instead? It is a possibility perhaps," agreed Jerry. "Do we have the money and how much would it cost, Mr Chairman of Finance?"

"Well," the Chairman of Finance replied, "if we are looking to own it outright that would be a long-term saving on no longer renting that sprawling parcel of land off Benton, so maybe a bank would look favourably on a proposal by us to buy land funded with a mortgage. Depends upon the numbers involved. I can't say off hand and it would be up to the bank in the end. But my committee could certainly put together a draft proposal."

"Could we fit in two new holes there?" asked someone.

"Jerry? Your call," invited Martin Cowmeadow.

"Well maybe. It's quite a tight spot though isn't it?"

"That small field alongside it also comes with the property, I happen to know," said Willoughby, his mind drifting back off scones and cream to the matter of the golf course.

"Does it?" said Jerry. "Then maybe something could be made to work if we knocked down the house. After what happened there I imagine everyone would approve of that – terrible business wasn't it – that'd give us a couple of extra short holes perhaps. At least that won't mean disturbing our good long holes. Hmm, we'd have to look at that. It's still not exactly ideal is it?"

"No, but this land is up for sale, so we could buy it," said the Chairman of Finance. "Well perhaps: depends if we can negotiate a price that we can afford. After what happened there, I doubt many people will be clamouring to buy it; and, indeed, it seems people are not. It could be the least worst of the options."

"Okay, well we have a way forward," said Jerry. "Sorry, I must dash. But my Greens Committee will look at seeing what we might be able to do with the land at Winnie's Place, in terms of creating two new holes on it and integrating these into the existing layout, and the Finance Committee can explore if we might be able to make the finances work. Thanks everyone for coming at such short notice. There'll have to be a meeting of the Heads of Committee to decide all this, but I thought it best it we got things moving as soon as possible. Oh, and please everyone, keep this just among ourselves at the moment – don't want to set off rumours and panic and goodness knows what. Nor, crucially, do we want Benton to find out what we are up to. So keep schtum folks."

"It might be a good idea," said Willoughby loudly as the group was breaking up, "if anyone who has got time to spare stay behind and barnstorm some ideas. Perhaps over scones and tea?"

"No need," said the Chairman of Estates, "we've already decided the next stage."

"Well maybe we could also discuss this new food card system," said Willoughby to the group, but everyone continued filing out, until only Willoughby was left.

"Good afternoon Sir," said the Steward approaching Willoughby, "would you like a drink?"

Chapter 4

The door of the committee room had been left open, and a head popped round it: "Ah, you're in here." Willoughby, who had been sitting alone inside the room, deep in thought, looked up. "Anun!" he cried delightedly, "what an unexpected delight."

"I've just popped in to the club to get my food and drink card," she explained, "and I saw your car and thought I'd come and say hallo, unless of course you were out on the course. But I thought you would probably be close to a food source instead," she said teasingly.

"I have already played the golf – with the padre," Willoughby said loftily.

"How did it go?"

"I was mildly magnificent."

"Who won?"

"It was either the vicar or me, but those are mere details that you should not trouble over."

"So the vicar won."

"And I came second. So we both did jolly well."

"So this is the committee room is it," said Anun looking around, "where all these great decisions of state are made. Such as whether sponge cake can be served before 4pm or not; or if mauve socks can be worn in the bar during the month of Lent if the person is left-handed and under six foot tall? I've never been in here before. It's not much to look at, is it?"

Willoughby looked around. It had never occurred to him before, but it was true. It was just four bare walls with a large table in the centre, with chairs around it. And that was it.

"I had expected paintings on the wall of stern, serious-looking men looking down on you all," continued Anun, "maybe some works of art commemorating the battle of the links, the match-winning putt which is still spoken of in revered tones through all the years; of stuffed heads hanging on the wall, maybe of a deer with magnificent antlers, or a previous chairman with a magnificent walrus moustache. Oh, will I get in trouble being in here, as merely a lowly social member? Will I be summoned to the Secretary's office and have the buttons cut off my club blazer with all the committee lined up outside turning their back on me one by one as I am marched through the car park? Oh, are you waiting for a committee meeting – should I scarper?"

"No, we have just had one. I am yet to leave after it. Shall we adjourn to the comfy chairs as my mother used to say after meals?"

"So I am being thrown out. I knew it would be too good to last this glimpse into the lives of the elite and the powerful."

"This is a treat to see you," said Willoughby as they walked from the room, "I thought you were away involved in educating young minds and bodies."

"I have been summoned home for a business conference," Anun replied.

"Now, you don't have a devious wife, do you," a happy thought having occurred to Willoughby.

"I don't have any sort of wife," Anun pointed out.

"Very wise, very wise, avoid getting one whatever you do."

"If you say so, Willoughby, then I will."

"Very wise. Oh, how's Bongo by the way?"

"Bingo. Oh, I've finished with him."

"Oh dear. Was it because he was a greedy pig who kept wolfing macaroons the whole time, so much so that he now looks much like a blobby human macaroon?"

"No, he was unfaithful."

"Was faithfulness important to you in the relationship?"

"His, yes."

"So you're single now are you?"

"No, I have a new fella, Felix." Then, laughing, she added: "Don't know why I told you his name."

"Why, is his name supposed to be a secret? You do go in for chaps with interesting names – old thingy and now um, whatshisname."

"What I meant is there's no point telling it to you, is there. You know what you're like with names – you always misremember them or forget them."

"I don't. That's a lie put out by Half Pint. She does fib so."

"Does she?"

"Yes, I just showed that I remembered your chap, well ex chap, the macaroon wolfer was called, um, Ludo didn't I?"

"I stand corrected."

"Is he very fat?"

"Who, Felix?"

"Who's Felix? No I meant Bongo, er Ludo. Bingo."

"No, still slim and muscular."

"Perhaps you can tell my wife next time you see her that Bingo spends morning, noon and night stuffing down macaroons and he is still slim and healthy."

"Why?"

"Well my wife seems to be under the impression that eating food is bad for you. Or, more specifically, that eating food is bad for me. I am surprised you even recognised me when you put your nose round the door."

"Well I have known you a long time – all my life I suppose in fact bar the first few months –"

"The saddest, emptiest months of your life, I am told," cut in Willoughby.

"– so I am hardly going to forget what you looked like."

"Yes, but I am but now a pale shadow of the man you once knew, the man I was when you last saw me. I am just a bag of bones in a loose-fitting skin."

"Well you look just the same well-rounded figure to me."

"You are just being kind and trying to keep my spirits up, and I salute you for it. But I clank now when I walk. I am just a skeleton in a loose disguise. I could be rented out for Halloween parties."

"You could go trick-or-treating," suggested Anun. "You'd like that as they give trick-or-treaters sweets and chocolate bars and suchlike. Maybe you could become a professional trick-or-treater? You are good at tricks."

"So you, who is fortunate in lacking a horrid, devious wife unlike some around here, can buy scones and cream with a pot of tea and whatever else the Steward may allow to be ordered before the sacred hour of 4pm."

"Is that what your committee meeting was about? Whether married men will be allowed food before 4pm?"

"I could tell you what the committee meeting was about, but then I would have to kill you."

"I would not like that."

"I would not like that either," said Willoughby.

"I would dislike it more, I think," replied Anun.

"You said you have a food and drink card. You can order food on it. Some scones would be lovely, Anun."

"I haven't got a card."

"You said you came in to collect it."

"I did. But the office was closed."

"So you haven't got a card?"

"No."

"Oh."

"So you will just have to order me some scones and tea

instead," said Anun brightly. "Some of Mummy's delicious scones and cream."

"I cannot," said Willoughby sadly. "My wife thinks I should not have any food. But I am all in favour of me having food. Unfortunately the card has taken her side in the argument."

"A food and drink card which does not allow you food? That seems an odd business decision by the club. Whose daft idea was that?"

"Rambo's it seems."

"Dumbo? Well, what can you expect? Can't you have a word with him and sort it out?"

"Well I did go round to tell him what, but, um, I didn't see him in the end. So neither of us two members can buy scones and cream at our own club."

"So it seems. I wonder if it ever occurs to anyone in that committee room to wonder how this club always seems to be cash strapped. Better not tell Mummy that people are being prevented from buying her wares. It won't cheer her."

"That's a point. What happens to the cakes she bakes before they come here, and how do they come here?"

"Harry brings him over and normally collects some crisps in exchange and takes them back. Why, are you thinking of becoming a highwayman and holding Harry up to steal the cakes as he makes his way along the lawless backstreets of Tangents? I'm not sure you'd get away with it as even in a mask you'd have a fairly distinctive profile. I think Harry would recognise you."

"You mean my chiselled features; the firm, craggy jawline?"

"Well, something like that."

Rambo, who had entered having heard rumours of an emergency committee meeting and was hanging around to see if it was true, while trying to make it seem that he was not hanging around, came across: "Sorry, I couldn't help overhearing, has there been another food theft?"

"These are lawless times Rambo," Willoughby replied sombrely. "Anun is thinking of sending Harry out only when accompanied by an armed guard, as there are rumours of a dastardly nefarious highwayman all set to operate in this area and planning to steal food from the local hard-working peasantry."

"There is! There is!" Rambo exclaimed excitedly. "He is here already, I had food stolen from me. Someone stole my lunch."

"A highwayman stole your lunch?" asked Anun.

"Yes, it sounds like him."

"Do you have witnesses?" asked Willoughby.

"No. But it was obviously the same person. It was earlier today and my wife had left my lunch on a tray outside my writing hut, as she does every day, and when I went to collect it, it had gone."

"She probably just forgot," said Willoughby.

"No, she remembered. What's more, I found the tray and plates later outside our house."

"Perhaps they had flown there?" suggested Willoughby.

"What? How could that have happened?"

"I don't know, as a wiser man than myself once said, I am but one of an advanced breed of monkeys on a minor planet of a very average star. But lots of respectable people have reported seeing flying saucers, so maybe there are flying plates as well? Stands to reason, if plates spend all their time hanging around with saucers they are bound to learn things from them. Or maybe they have got jealous of all those milk jugs which seem to end up flying about the place whenever you're around? Either way, it rather suggests that they have not been stolen if you still have them."

"But the food on the plates had all gone. The food has been stolen don't you see!"

"Probably foxes."

"Do foxes use a knife and fork?"

"Aaah-ummm, well. Sure you hadn't eaten it absent mindedly? You know how you writers can be. William Shakespeare was notorious for it. He was always accusing Anne Hathaway for being late bringing him his lunch and she would retort that he'd already eaten it. Indeed, one day when he was working on Hamlet he was wondering if he had eaten or whether to be angry with her or not, and absent mindedly he wrote down 'to be, or not to be that is the question', and it accidentally ended up in the published version of the play script. He was never entirely sure she still wasn't diddling him out of his lunch some days, and Shakespearean scholars have speculated that this is why he only left her his second-best bed in his will. You probably wolfed down your lunch when you were wrestling with a badly behaved semi colon and it took your mind off what you were eating."

"No, no, it was stolen I tell you! And now you say Harry has come under danger of having his food stolen. Well the club's food stolen. This is terrible. We must stop this. We must do something. This is terrible. I must tell the police. Has Harry told the police?" demanded Rambo.

"I believe M15 and MI6 have been informed," said Willoughby sombrely.

"MI5, M16? What use is that? He should have contacted the local police. I must tell the police," and with that Rambo rushed off self-importantly.

"Is there something you want to share with the class, Willoughby?" asked Anun.

"What is the class studying? Geography? If so, I used to be able to recite the capital cities of countries: it was my party piece when I was young. I have lots of facts about capitals to educate your class. Do you know that Wales did not have a capital city until 1965, for instance?"

"No, about who stole Dumbo's lunch."

"Oh that. All rather far-fetched wasn't it. Sounds like a classic insurance scam to me."

"One way to lose weight is to take plenty of exercise," said Anun, "so what are you doing driving to the club? Especially as I thought you usually walked everywhere around the village?"

"Yes, well I have to take the car now because of that cattle grid. You know the one."

"Yes, of course I do – we have to walk over it to get here. I don't know if you've ever tried walking over a cattle grid in high heels."

"No, can't say that I have."

"Well don't attempt it."

"I won't."

"You won't forget the experience. Or that there is a cattle grid there. Nor would you forget it if you have ever tried to clamber over a stile in a long ball dress."

"What a full life you have," said Willoughby, "or maybe I just have an empty one. Bit like my stomach."

"What's your stomach got to do with it?"

"It's empty. If you were to pick me up and shake me all you would hear is the rattling of a few sesame seeds. That is what my meals at home consist of these days, a handful, well a fingerful, of sesame seeds and half a grape or, if my wife is feeling in a particularly bountiful mood, three-quarters of grape. It's very sad. Not just for me, but for all those unborn sesame trees. Have you ever seen a sesame tree in the wild? No? Course not. That's because they never get the chance to be born, to be planted, to grow to experience life and to reach for the skies. Instead they are getting aborted by mad food faddists and end up rattling around people's stomachs."

"I don't think they are that sort of seed," said Anun.

"I wonder what a sesame tree looks like anyway? It could of course be that they are terribly ugly things, or maybe they are like hawthorns and are total pricks, so perhaps I am grieving for them unnecessarily. Better see if I can borrow Half Pint's Boy's Bumper Book of British Trees that I got her all those years ago – or was it the Girl's Ginormous Guide to Great Trees – that might tell me."

"Hey, you haven't yet explained why you have to go in the car because of that cattle grid," Anun reminded him.

"Oh well now I'm so thin, basically just a human version of a sheet of paper, I daren't risk going over it as I'll most likely slip down between the gratings never to be seen again, or be this poor weak feeble voice crying out from the depths of the pit below. Hoping my sad, bleating cries do not get confused as the chatter of the neighbouring sheep and ignored by others walking over it."

"I don't think your figure has exactly got to that stage yet," said Anun.

"Almost. It is not long now until you will be able to fold me up and send me anywhere in the world for the cost of a first-class stamp. I can't even sleep with the window open any more as if there is the lightest gust of wind I get blown out of bed. The other day I was having a dream when I was floating and I woke up and found it was perfectly true: I was. I was very fortunate I didn't get wafted out of the window or goodness knows where I would have ended up."

"Couldn't Mrs C have caught you and dragged you down?"

"Although she is good at dragging me down, she was not there. We have long since ceased such intimacy."

"Oh dear, is it so very awful for you?" said Anun.

"It is; it is," said Willoughby, nodding sorrowfully.

"Maybe I can have a word with your good lady wife and sort something better out."

"I am no bigamist," said Willoughby shaking his head, "I have but the one wife. But you haven't said what has dragged you back from the groves of academe. What is this business conference – are you addressing the CBI or something?"

"Mummy has had an approach from a housebuilder to buy some of our land, and she is pondering it and wanted to discuss it with us. She is finding the farm too large for her to get around and look after since her accident, but she doesn't really fancy the idea of having houses on our doorstep. Nor me: I do like the vista of looking out over our lands, modest as they may be, and across to the golf course in the distance. But it would be income, and Mummy does need that."

"Well it wouldn't really be income would it, rather just a one-off cash injection."

"Yes, that is rather my view, too. And that is my main worry – what does it leave? If the smallholding becomes too small to be a practical proposition for someone else to take on, does selling off some land for housing cause as many problems as it solves?"

"'For someone else to take on?'" Willoughby queried.

"Well Mummy is going to retire one day and I don't want to take the thing on and, well, Rikki might want to – but it's been a struggle for Mummy most years I think to make ends meet and so would one really wish that future on Rikki? Should she move away and have a proper career in something elsewhere?"

"Rikki leave Tangents? That'd be awful. I mean, she wouldn't like that."

"Well I don't think she wants to, but what is the alternative? If Mummy sells this land that leaves less land to work and would that size a holding ever be profitable or an attractive proposition to a buyer down the line? Mummy's looking to diversify. The baking for the club is a good start, but it is only a modest income. That is the idea behind converting that outbuilding into accommodation that Harry's cousin is helping with. Mummy was thinking it could maybe be accommodation for a bed and breakfast business, or for holiday rentals, or maybe just for a farm worker to stay in as, if Rikki and I move out, she loses her unpaid workforce. Harry's okay as a stop gap but I don't think he sees his future as Paddock's unpaid farm hand in return for free board and lodging."

"No, I have sussed that."

"How's his writing going?"

"Well enough that he will need free board and lodging for a while yet."

"Oh dear. Well oh dear for him that is. But every cloud and so on. Rikki's coming home too, by the way."

"If she's passing this way, tell her I'm hard to find nowadays being such a tiny figure. But tell her to look me up, if she's got the time. She here for the conference?"

"Well the conference is more timed to coincide with her coming back. She is coming to say farewell to Rik-pig, who is going away."

"Off on his hols is he, touring the football stadia of Europe or something?"

"No, as this little piggy went to market."

"Oh. I see."

"Yes, he could be one of your meals shortly."

"Why, is he being turned into sesame seeds? I may be a simple country bumpkin, but it has always struck me as ironic how some farmers can profess to love some living thing yet are planning to kill them. Mind you, my wife seems to have the same philosophy. Oh dear, Harry will be upset."

"He doesn't actually like the pig does he?"

"Not in itself, no. I think mild indifference is the most one could claim. But he is trying to curry favour with Rikki. Curry," said Willoughby, his mind going off on a tangent. "My wife used to make a good curry, you know. Now what was I saying? Very nice curry: not too spicy and full of flavour. Oh yes, Harry is hoping the pig would put in a good word for him with Half Pint. You know, when the pig writes to her at uni or however it keeps in touch. Harry has even been teaching it the offside law. Complete waste of time of course, because even if the pig learns it there is no way the pig would be able to explain it to Half Pint. She never understands anything to do with sport. Oh dear, what will happen to the club's cheese-and-onion crisp mountain if Rik-pig is no longer there to munch through it all."

"It has all gone, Harry reports. Or will have shortly: Harry carried the last box of crisps home today. Rik-pig has munched through the whole lot."

"Cor, rather it than me."

"Don't you like crisps?"

"No."

"Gosh, I didn't think there was any food you dislike," she said teasingly.

"This shows you are wrong, smarty-pants. Oh yes, there are some, crisps being a case in point. Can't see the point of them. Salt and vinegar are just about tolerable if tangy, but the rest of them: no thanks. And cheese and onion: yuck!"

"Are you free tomorrow evening?"

"Yes, why are you throwing a dinner party?" asked Willoughby hopefully.

"No, but Rikki will be here then, so we could pootle over and have a drink with you here, if you like."

"I'd like that very much."

"Right: that's what we'll do. Well lovely though it has been not having scones and cream with you, I better go back and see if I am needed to help Mummy prepare for her houseful, or if I am needed as a chippy's mate or whatever."

As he was about to get into his car to leave, Willoughby was hailed by someone. He looked around and it was Marmaduke, marching towards him with a bag of clubs over his shoulder.

"Oh hallo again," said Willoughby, "you just off for a quick knock with Harry?"

"No, I've left Harry beavering away. I've just nipped out as I was hoping to see if I could get a quick nine holes in. I've borrowed Harry's clubs," he said patting them. "If I play the front nine does that get me back to the clubhouse?"

"No, it does not, it will take you down to the halfway hut," Willoughby replied. Then the mention of the hut gave him an idea: "Oh, if you haven't got any company, I'll happily play nine holes with you to the halfway hut. If you don't know our course I can guide you round, but it's fairly straightforward."

"Well that is very kind, I'd be glad to have your company," replied Marmaduke.

"Splendid, just a tick and I'll get my clubs out of the boot," said Willoughby. "Sorry, we don't have a putting green or anything if you wanted a warm up, so we'll just go to the 1st tee. There's unlikely to be anyone around at this time."

Chapter 5

"Okay," said Willoughby on the 1st tee. "Fairly gentle opening shot as you can see. The hole bends round to the left, so favour the right of the fairway if anything. The thing to watch out for here is the approach shot as this flagstick is shorter than the rest, so don't get tricked into thinking you are further from the hole than you actually are."

"Why is this flag shorter?" asked Marmaduke, partly out of curiosity, partly to make conversation.

"You can't see the green from here, but you'll see it's on a wee hilltop and so is a bit exposed and when the wind blows hard we found that a normal-height flagstick could get blown down, so now we have a shorter one. Would you like the honour?"

"No, you can lead us off," said Marmaduke, waving Willoughby forward. "You can show me how to do it."

Willoughby's drive soared away straight down the middle. "Oh where is the vicar now," he said, surveying his effort with pride laced with a modicum of surprise.

"Sorry?" said Marmaduke.

"Sorry, talking to myself really. I am playing with the padre tomorrow in a club competition, the Bowler's Name it's called, as the names were drawn out of a bowler hat. Or would have been had we a bowler hat. Quite a fun idea we hope – a better ball competition where there is a draw for partners. I got drawn with the vicar, which was a form of irony as he is my regular partner. Well now he is; it was Godders for, well, oh so many years," his voice tailed off into silence before Willoughby recovered himself with: "and, well, let us say I did not put on my best performance this morning, and I'm not entirely sure the vicar was overly impressed nor overly optimistic about our performance tomorrow – we are playing at crack of dawn as he has a Diocesan lunch to go to, lucky devil. Mind you, if you saw his putting today: shocking!"

Marmaduke topped his tee shot, which scuttled along the fairway – but not for long. "Dead straight," said Willoughby approvingly, accentuating the positive.

"The idea behind the competition is to shake things up a bit," continued Willoughby. "So often at a golf club like ours people play in their own close-knit groups and so don't get to know or socialise with most of the other members. Clubs can so easily descend into a collection of different coteries and cliques. Can't really avoid that, I suppose, but this competition was designed to get people playing with other members, actually playing with them, rather than simply alongside, so as to form some bonds between people and help encourage new friendships, connections; well, just really to open up some of the social groups. We had the draw in the clubhouse one evening last week and invited everyone along to it who had entered for the draw. We had to do that so that people would know who they had been drawn to play with, as they might not know the other person. The first person in the team stood up when their name was pulled out of the hat, and the second person did so when they got drawn out – made it seem a bit like a scene in these westerns which used to be on telly when I was a kid. It was a great fun social evening really, people getting to know one another, finding out their partner, arranging a game with their opponents – it's a knockout you see. We really should create more occasions like that to shake things up."

"Another advantage of having it in the clubhouse," Willoughby chuckled, "was that we knew Benton would not participate as he is still boycotting it, and we knew if the threat of potentially being drawn to play with Benton existed this new competition would be dead in the water."

"This Benton Snivelgate not popular here then?"

"Do you know him? Friend of yours?"

"No. I have never met him. But Dad was involved with him at one stage. Some business venture or other."

"Your father works with him?"

"No, nothing came of it in the end; don't know why. But the name obviously stuck in the dark recesses of my mind – it's quite an unusual name – so when you said Benton Snivelgate it triggered it. What's Benton Snivelgate like? Not popular, I take it?"

"A louse of the highest order. Or should that be of the lowest order? Your father dodged a bullet there."

"Oh," said Marmaduke before addressing his second shot, which he also topped.

"Again, dead straight," said Willoughby encouragingly of a shot that had sent the ball trundling without any display of fervour or enthusiasm a short way further down the fairway in the approximate direction of the hole. Willoughby decided now would not be a good moment to ask the standard, if unoriginal, question as to where the other usually plays their golf, that he had come armed with when playing with this stranger. Instead he fell back on that other fallback of conversation, the other's work. "So, you are a carpenter?"

"Well more by accident than design that is what I have become. So, yes, I suppose so. My father has a building company and all of us sons were set to work in school holidays in helping out and a young me – I'm the youngest son – was set some of the basic carpentry tasks, such as banging in nails, as they thought I could not mess up and well it sort of developed from there. I do enjoy carpentry and, though I say it myself, I've got quite good at it, but it's not really what I want to do with my life. In fact it's definitely not what I want to all my life. I don't want to spend my life on my knees."

"You want to walk tall through life," suggested Willoughby.

"Well I don't want to end up working all my life in the family firm. As the youngest brother, there is no progression for me. My eldest brother will be the one who'll inherit the managing director position in due course, and me and my eldest brother don't see eye-to-eye on many things. He sees life through a spreadsheet. I have an artistic appreciation of things of which he is devoid. I want us to build beautiful, imaginative houses, whereas he just wants to churn out something functional as cheaply as possible."

"So what do you want to do instead?" asked Willoughby.

"Well I've grown up amongst the building trade and property so I think 'stick to what you know'. But what I really love and what really fascinates me is the landscaping aspect, the interaction of man and landscape and how buildings can react and relate to a natural world in their settings and surroundings. That's how I got interested in golf in the first place. It is not a great fascination in hitting a ball into a hole in as few shots as possible," he said, breaking off from what he was saying to play his third shot.

"That's probably just as well," said Willoughby, as Marmaduke's shot spluttered away apologetically about 45 degrees off his intended target line.

"Sorry I'm a bit rusty. I'm normally a bit better than this – not a lot, but a bit," said Marmaduke cheerfully. "No, my interest in golf worked backwards from the landscape angle. I was walking across a golf course one day, and it struck me here is living, breathing man-made landscape which serves a defined purpose, but which also contrives to look a natural, organic part of the environment and that intrigued me on, well, almost an intellectual level I suppose, and that drew me in to the game. How the holes set their own individual challenges and then combine in a different way to set a collective challenge. How the holes flow from one to another, how you bring about contrast and drama. When it's done well, it's a beautiful work of art. I got further and further drawn into it, reading about the great golf architects, their theories and philosophies.

"Where I grew up there was a driving range and a short course. The driving range was obviously the main focus and the money spinner. There was also a short nine-hole course. The land was flat with the holes mainly running parallel to one another and separated by rows of lollipop trees, and I thought it the most sterile, barren environment. That had put me off golf. It's a crying shame people build such unimaginative courses – okay, they had an excuse, it was a place for beginners and the course probably served its purpose of introducing people to the game. But it is a shame that you sometimes see mediocre courses laid out over inviting land which would have been so receptive to a better, more vibrant design.

"I started to play golf so as to inform my study of golf-course design. Or modern landscaping as I think of it as. When younger, I used to be fascinated with those great garden designers who laid out the gardens and grounds of country houses. Well, who even now puts even a modest-sized garden with modern houses? It's a tablecloth-worth of lawn, perhaps soon to be eaten into by decking or a cheap extension of a conservatory tacked on to a house. There's no canvas to work with there for a landscaper, but a hundred or more acres of land to lay out a golf course, that offers scope, the chance for imagination, flair, drama, beauty, visual tricks, whatever. It's fascinating – well to me, anyway. Sorry, I am going on."

"No, please do, dear boy. This is all most interesting. I can see why kneeling on the ground hammering in floorboards may not give you the same thrill."

"My dream job," continued Marmaduke, "well, my dream scenario would be designing and building a new village somewhere in sympathy and harmony to the surroundings. Houses that provide great living accommodation, but which are fun to look at, and make statements about beauty and elegance. It will probably never happen, but that would be my dream."

"I wish you luck with that," said Willoughby, as Marmaduke settled down to play his fourth shot, which he sent soaring towards the green. "Oh good shot," said Willoughby. I think you've held the green: great result. So what are you doing to take you towards this dream?"

"Well I know I will have to do it away from the family firm. So I am looking to set up on my own, but before that I need to have some actual work or projects to do, so I am scouting around to see if there are any opportunities."

Willoughby duffed his next shot. "Perhaps just as well the vicar isn't here," he remarked. But then he played a superb chip and putted out for par. Marmaduke three putted.

"Your hole, Sir," said Marmaduke.

"Oh there's no need for any of that: we're just a couple of pals playing round. But yes, that is me one up."

They continued round the course, as the light slowly ebbed from the day. Willoughby was enjoying himself, learning about Marmaduke and listening with interest as Marmaduke talked of landscaping with relation to golf courses, picking up little aspects of the design of the course at Tangents that Willoughby had only been dimly or subconsciously aware of. As Willoughby was also playing uncommonly well for him, he was having a fine time of it, especially as he knew the crowning glory would be that all this was leading to the halfway hut, where he would be able to get some of the rudiments of afternoon tea. He was slightly concerned that Marmaduke would hold them up, as he was taking a lot of shots on most holes, but Marmaduke walked quickly and did not waste time over his shots.

"Oh, what's that over there?" asked Marmaduke pointing in the distance. "It looks like something in the process of being dismantled?"

"That's the greenkeeping shed, and it's not so much been dismantled as fallen down. We needed a new shed and, as this club is perpetually strapped for cash, we launched a 10-year membership scheme to pay for it, which was not a great success. Then Benton said he knew someone who could build it cheaply for us, and, well, they did not do a good job. Seem to have done it too cheaply, cut too many corners and one windy night it came crashing down. Fortunately, it was during the night so no one was in it."

"Oh gosh," said Marmaduke. "That is not good." Willoughby looked across at him and saw that Marmaduke was looking thoughtful and perhaps even a bit shocked.

"You spying a building opportunity there?"

"Er, no, why do you say that?"

"Well a shed needs building; you want to start your own building company – there seems to be a two-and-two situation there."

"Oh! I see what you mean. Oh, that's an interesting idea. Thank you. Who would I need to speak to? Is it this er Benton Snivelgate fellow you were talking about?"

"Benton? No fear. He is nothing to do with the running of the club."

"Oh it is just that you said he'd organised the building of the shed."

"Goodness knows why they let him do that. They were just desperate I suppose. But they're certainly not going to make that mistake again. Would you want to work with a chap who had done that? No, it would be, hmm, I suppose it would be the Estates Committee, or would it be the Greens Committee you'd need to speak to? Or maybe it's Finance Committee? Don't think it would come under the Heads of Committee's remit. Or is it General Purposes?"

When they came to the 9th hole Willoughby said: "Last one, then perhaps a stop off at the halfway hut. It does not have the full range of items that the clubhouse does, and it's geared to the golfer, so no scones and cream; just things which can be eaten without cutlery. It's not run by the club but by a lovely little old lady. She's quite an old lady now. She's been doing it for years. But she gets some of the stuff from Mrs Winsor as well. The variety and quality of the offering has gone up a lot since Mrs Winsor has been involved. We get all sorts now. Martin Cowmeadow is a big fan of the Chorley cakes here. We don't always get those, depends what Mrs Winsor has baked. Sometimes we get flapjacks, parkin, brownies, we had gingerbread men once, very imaginative they were – styled as golfers. She is very artistic, Mrs Winsor. She paints as well. She had a show of her works recently. You never know quite what delights will be on offer here, it's always a joyous surprise to find out what they are. There are also things like sausage rolls, sausage baps, if you want some hot food, or chocolate bars, plus hot and cold drinks – all that sort of thing."

After they had played the ninth hole, Willoughby said "Do you wish something from the halfway hut? I think I will stop and have an ersatz afternoon tea."

"That is very kind," replied Marmaduke, "but if you don't mind I think I will plough on and see if I can get in the 10th and 11th holes. But please don't let me stop you having your tea. I can play on my own. Thank you so much for showing me round the course. It has been most interesting."

"Don't worry, you won't stop me," said Willoughby, marching with great happiness towards the halfway hut.

When he got there, he saw a sign on the door: "Closed for funeral."

Chapter 6

Willoughby sat down with a thud on one of the benches outside the halfway hut, reeling from this latest piece of outrageous fortune adding one more chapter to his tea of troubles. That would have been why the office was closed, he reflected: Miss Murtle would have been helping out with the catering at the funeral, as she was holding the fort after whatshername, Mrs Roach, who used to look after the church catering, had handed in her dinner pail.

He got up and tried the door just in case it had been left unlocked as then he could go in and help himself and leave some money on the counter. The door was locked. He looked fleetingly at the windows, but this was more a sign of his desperation in his sadness as he already knew full well that, even if he could have somehow prised one of the windows open, a man of his size and age was not going to clamber easily through one – he did not fancy being discovered like Winnie The Pooh stuck in Rabbit's front door when Mrs French came to unlock her hut in the morning.

He sat back down on the bench with another hefty thud. He looked across to the 10th hole. He saw that Marmaduke had not got far down that fairway. But then he had learnt that Marmaduke tended to take things in stages when hitting a ball down the length of a hole, a bit at a time, creeping up on the green gradually as though to catch it unawares. Willoughby wondered whether he should join him, but he had no appetite for more golf now that he no longer had the lure of the halfway hut pulling him on. Marmaduke was wandering around in a manner which looked unfocused from a distance, suggesting that he had lost his ball and, moreover, had lost sight of where it had set out towards. Sometimes that can happen, and golfers just do not pick up the flight of his shot at all and have only to go off the feel of the shot. Maybe that had happened to Marmaduke. Willoughby wondered that, if Marmaduke was now hitting the ball far enough that he could lose it, it meant he was getting better or worse.

Willoughby also wondered whether he should go over and help Marmaduke in his search. But he had little enthusiasm for that, so told himself that Marmaduke would not wish attention drawn to yet another errant shot; not that Marmaduke, by his own cheerful testimony, had any pretensions of being much of a golfer. The unusual route Marmaduke had taken to becoming a golfer had intrigued Willoughby. His own route to the game had been that the golf course was somewhere where his mother could take him in the school holidays and leave him knowing that he would be safe and have something to do. After all these years, Willoughby could no longer remember whether the original suggestion that he take up golf had been his or his parents' one, or something just mutually arrived at.

It was at the golf club that he had first met Godfrey Flower. Willoughby had always presumed that Godders' parents had had much the same idea as his own, as Godfrey was also on his tod. The two of them had palled up and played together through those summer holidays. Having got into the habit of playing together as children they had carried on doing so throughout their lives; well, throughout Godders' life.

Willoughby's mother would always give him some money for a bottle of pop after the game, which he would have while waiting to be collected. Willoughby would share this money with Godfrey, so his mother began leaving him some more money so he could buy Godfrey a drink as well, once she realised he had palled up with another child. When Godfrey's parents heard that he was being bought drinks by another child, they started giving Godfrey money so he could buy him and his friend drinks. So often both children would come armed with money for two drinks each. The golfers decided they would play matches with the loser paying for the drinks and the winner getting to keep their money. Willoughby laughed at the recollection. That the loser paid for the drinks had become Godfrey's and his thing: it had continued into adult life.

No silly card systems in those days. No halfway hut either. He looked up at the halfway hut, which he realised was beginning to show its years, something he had not noticed before or, if he had, it had not registered with him. He tried to remember when the hut was built – it had not been a feature of the course when he and Godfrey spent those summer holidays playing golf together. He could not place now exactly when it had come into being. It was a wooden shack which in the early days did not have this covered verandah. It was a very basic construction back then: it had started out as something akin to an overgrown sentry box. The idea of a seating area came later; originally you had simply gone to a hatch where you could order hot or cold drinks or from a small selection of chocolate bars. It had been run at first by a married couple, a mousy woman and a man of stern countenance who was, on reflection, more friendly than he had looked.

They had not lasted long; well, a few years, and then Mrs French and her sister took it over and had run it ever since. Well Mrs French had; her sister had given up when her husband retired and the pair of them had moved elsewhere to be nearer their daughter and grandchildren. The food offering had improved when the sisters took over. Willoughby thought it was them who had introduced hot food as he couldn't remember the previous couple offering that. They certainly introduced baked goods as the sister liked to bake. She made some superb flapjacks Willoughby remembered: beautifully moist, syrupy and chewy. When she retired, Mrs Winsor had stepped in as the supplier of baked goods, and the food offering had never been so good. The service though had got worse as it was just Mrs French now soldiering on alone in the halfway hut and she was herself slowing down.

He got up to walk back, noticing as he did so that Marmaduke had seemingly abandoned the 10th hole and was now walking straight to the 11th tee.

As Willoughby walked back across the course he thought about what Marmaduke had been saying about golfing landscapes. It had been instructive to see the course through another's perceptive eyes. He realised that he had never really considered the course like this. When he was young, the golf course was just there, something you played over without questioning it. He had got more interested in matters of golf-course design when he started playing different courses, but he never really applied it to Tangents. Tangents was just an old friend, someone whose looks and quirks you had got used to and never questioned or really thought about. It had changed little since those distant days, or maybe it had changed a lot, just in incremental ways that he hadn't noticed or had forgotten about now, just as all his other friends' looks had changed over the decades, incrementally and imperceptibly.

As he walked down the 8th fairway, he thought of the bunker which used to be there which had caused Godfrey so many problems for so many years. He wished it was still there or, if it had to go, it had gone when Godfrey still played the course. Marmaduke's entertaining chatter still running round his head, Willoughby reflected on how the course was a landscape he had interacted with over the decades, and the memories it held for him; comforting, pleasing memories on the whole. It was a happy, familiar place, a constant relationship through the years. Had you asked him about the club, he would have thought of the people, his friends, the companionship. But he realised that the course itself was also part of this emotional relationship.

He also thought, as he walked through the gathering gloom of the evening, how that was also going to be disturbed if the 10th and 11th holes were to go. Or did they keep them to preserve the integrity of the course? But could they afford to – the club was perpetually cash strapped. Was trying to maintain an 18-hole course on the outskirts of a large village in the middle of nowhere an unrealistic proposition in the modern world? Was it just an act of vanity even? Sixteen holes would look a bit sad, a public sign that they had had 18 holes, but failed to hold on to them. Maybe they should drop down to nine, and sell the remainder of their land for development? Maybe the club should redevelop the land itself, to preserve the surrounds of the course in an attractive manner. He thought of courses he had played, good in themselves, but marred by being surrounded by ugly or intrusive architecture. If the club sold the land, or developed it and sold the subsequent housing, that could solve the club's financial problems once and for all. Though it would then be a different club. But then a worse club was better than no club, and if the club were to go, so would much of Tangents' life. Or was there another way to be found that Tangents could continue as an 18-hole course?

He was aware that, having wrong footed himself about what the emergency committee meeting was about, he had not fully interacted with it. Which, in turn, brought him back to the pressing practical consideration of where he was going to get some form of afternoon tea.

Brian often spent afternoons in an armchair in the club doing the crossword, maybe he could be persuaded to buy him a spot of afternoon tea. But Brian was not someone interested in afternoon tea. Few were. Rikki and the vicar were his usual companions for afternoon tea and one was at uni and the other was conducting a funeral service, or had been as it would be well over by now. It would be the funeral tea he would be at. No, even that would probably be finished by now. That gave Willoughby an idea, and he set out for the church.

There were no signs of the funeral when he got to the church but, as Willoughby had expected, the vicar was still there, pottering about the place.

"Hallo padre."

"Willoughby – what brings you here?"

"I have been playing golf."

"I know. It was me you were playing with. Remember?"

"No, been playing again with er, Marmaduke."

"Who's Marmaduke? If that is actually his name."

"Why would he give me a false name?"

"No, it is… no matter."

"He is Larry's cousin. Come to help convert that outbuilding at Paddock's Farm. A carpenter with dreams. I played very well. I thought you'd like to know that I have been getting in some practice for our match tomorrow morning. Meant I had to forgo my afternoon tea though. I don't suppose there is anything knocking about here?"

"This is a church not a cafeteria. The best I can offer here is a communion wafer. At the next communion service."

"Nothing left over from the funeral tea looking for a good home. I was just thinking, thrift, thrift and how the funeral baked meats could have furnished the cold marriage dining table."

"No. Is that why you came?"

"Oh no, just thought I'd pop in en route home to tell you that my form had taken an upturn."

"But the church is not on your route home."

"I am in the car," said Willoughby by way of explanation.

"Maybe, but it still isn't on your way home."

"It is when I come via the church. This Diocesan lunch of yours. How do people get invited to that?"

"Well it typically starts off with the person having a chat with the local vicar."

"Excellent, excellent."

"Then the vicar, if he or she thinks the person suitable, would recommend that person to the Diocesan Director of Ordinands, who would conduct several interviews with the person, and probably ask them to read and review some books, write some essays, that sort of thing. If the DDO is impressed by the person, the DDO will arrange some interviews with the Bishop's advisers and if, after this, they are also of the belief that the person may be suitable they will tell the Bishop. The Bishop will then invite the person to attend a three-day residential conference. If they still deem the person suitable following this, that person is invited to enrol in a theological college for three years of study after which they apply to be a curate and, after a least a year as a curate, they would then be eligible to be appointed a vicar, and if they are appointed a vicar to a church in this diocese then they get invited to the lunch."

"Seems a lot of effort for one lunch. Is it a good lunch?"

"Not particularly. Normally just soup and sandwiches." The ensuing silence was broken by the vicar remembering: "Oh dear, the Dean will be at it."

"Why is that a problem? Is he someone who slurps his soup?"

"No, he was very impressed, as you know, with my outreach work at this church and he wants to know what I have planned next."

"What do you have planned next?"

"Nothing. The only thing that has come across my desk, well pushed through the vicarage door by some unseen hand, was an invitation from an organisation offering to give a lecture on burglary prevention. It's by some former policemen who apparently go round giving a talk offering tips to deter burglars. I wasn't sure that is a thing for the church, especially when I don't know who had put it my way either. I found it on the doormat one day when I got home and as I had passed Benton in the lane just before then I wondered if he had delivered it. I asked if it was him next time I saw him, but he said it wasn't."

"If Benton may be involved I think it is best avoided. You could perhaps put on some church lunches?" suggested Willoughby.

"That's no good. That would just be the existing congregation coming together. Need to be things which will attract people beyond the regular attendees at church. I have also had the Secretary on at me."

"The Dean's secretary?"

"No, Pirbright. He wants me to outline what I am doing as chaplain of the golf club."

"Are you doing anything?"

"No."

"Well that should be quite simple to outline."

"His inference, I took it, was that he thought I should be doing more as the club was in effect paying me the equivalent of a membership sub."

"I thought you are there to be consulted by members, if needed, on spiritual matters and to show the club is connected to the local community."

"I thought so, too."

"Perhaps you could institute prayer breakfasts?"

"Would people come to those?"

"Well I'd come along. So long as you didn't serve sesame seeds."

"The club doesn't serve breakfasts. The kitchen isn't open then."

"Well scrap that then. Perhaps you could revive the Taste of Tangents?"

"What on earth is that? I have never heard of it."

"Oh. It was a long time ago. A long time, well before your time. Before my time even. I remember my grandmother telling me about it."

"Well what is it?"

"Well-ahhmm. As I said, I remember my grandmother talking about it when I was very young. It was something that happened in her youth. People in the village would bake something and the official Taster of Tangents would go round to their house and taste it."

"Seems an odd thing. What's it got to do with the church?"

"Well the vicar came too. It was the Taster and the vicar who went." Willoughby saw that the vicar was now looking more interested.

"But why?"

"Well I rather suspect the general idea behind the Taste of Tangents was that it was a sort of marriage bureau. It was a way of advertising someone's suitability as a potential wife. Show off their cooking ability. It was handy perhaps if you had a daughter without obvious scenic properties but who was a good cook."

"Oh, like your wife... like your wife if she had a daughter she wanted to marry off but who wasn't catching the eye of the local youth, this was a way for her perhaps to do it?"

"Yes. And perhaps even those who turned a shapely ankle had to take part to show they were not all style over substance as it were."

"But why was the vicar involved?"

"Well everything tended to revolve around the church more in those days didn't it. But I guess the vicar was there to, as it were, give the seal of approval of the lady's moral character and the Taster of her culinary skills."

"But what did they do? Post a list at the parish pump of those who had passed the test or something?"

"No, it was part of some festival occasion and this was, well, the way you qualified to take part I suppose. It continued over two Sundays. The first Sunday the er, qualifying villagers I suppose you could call them took their ingredients, or their cooking utensils or something and had them blessed at a church service and told to make their food with gladness and a joyful heart for God approves of what they are doing and then the following week there was a tea when their wares were presented which the villagers who had come to the service could sample. That would be your outreach work, padre, in getting people into your church two weeks running."

"Yes indeed," said the vicar enthused. "It still strikes me as a very odd thing. I have never heard of this before."

"Well it was a long time ago. Things were different then. And all villages have their odd traditions don't they: whether it's chasing down a hill after a piece of cheese, pancake races, burning tar carrying, wife carrying –"

"Wife carrying?"

"Yes, a village in Surrey has an annual wife-carrying race over a 400-yard course dotted with obstacles and the spectators fire water pistols and chuck buckets of water at the competitors as they go by and the winner gets a barrel of ale and the loser a tin of dog food, and the chap who carries the heaviest wife gets a string of sausages if he completes the course. If you have a very petite wife you have to carry a rucksack full of baked bean tins as well as her."

"I don't believe there can be any such thing. Would any husband or wife subject themselves to such a thing? Would you do it Willoughby?"

"No, not even for a string of sausages."

"I think you are allowing your power of invention to carry you away again, Willoughby. But back to the Taste of Tangents: there can't have been many people taking part if it was just the young maidens of the village."

"I think others took part. The new wives did so to show what good wives they had become. I think an element of, well you might almost call it swank was involved. Or perhaps a feeling that if you did not take part the gossips might start speculating as to what you had to hide?"

"Who appointed the Taster?"

"No idea," said Willoughby.

"Would it be the vicar?"

"Dunno."

"Was this Taste of Tangents an annual event?"

"Not sure. I got the impression that it wasn't a one-off, so I guess so. But I dunno."

"Was a different Taster appointed each year, if so?"

"Sorry, all the finer details I am ignorant of. I am sure if you spoke to Rambo he would tell you all about it in copious and exacting detail, as he must have come across it in his research into the history of Tangents."

"No, no that's quite all right," said the vicar, "I am sure that details like that don't matter. Anyway any revival would not have to be an exact copy of the original. That would be something anyway to say to the Dean tomorrow if he asks. I am sure what you say is correct. But I shall look through the old church records to see what mentions of it I can find – that might provide some more details."

"Delighted if it will help you tomorrow with the Dean," said Willoughby. "Always happy to help you, padre. If I can help out in any other way, be happy to offer my services. Oh, and if you need someone to be the Taster I'd happily help out there."

"That's very public-spirited of you, Willoughby," said the vicar, smiling.

After Willoughby bade the vicar goodbye, he thought perhaps he should see Rambo to talk to him about the Taste of Tangents. He had an idea that Rambo might be in the clubhouse – as indeed he was. "Ah Rambo, I was just having a chat with the vicar about the Taste of Tangents."

"What on earth is that?"

"Ha-ha. you and your little jokes, Rambo. Good try, but you can't fool me. As I said to the vicar, you would know all about it of course being the local historian. Wouldn't be much cop as a local historian, I said to the vicar, if he didn't know about the Taste of Tangents, one of the most significant events in the village's dim and distant history. The vicar and I were chatting about it and there were some questions we didn't know the answer to, but I said I was sure you would know all the details as it had once upon a time been a big thing locally."

"When?" asked Rambo with aggressive suspicion.

"Oh yonks ago; yonks ago squared even – it was when my grandmother was a young girl. I think. Round that time."

"What was it?" asked Rambo.

"Why don't you know? Surely if anyone should know all about the Taste of Tangents it's you. It was quite a big thing in its day, the vicar was saying. I remember my grandmother telling me about it when I was young."

"Well I know something about it. Of course I do. But why don't you tell me all you know and I will see if I can fill in the gaps in your knowledge."

Willoughby told Rambo what he had told the vicar about it, and said how they were thinking of reviving it, "which of course would be of interest to you as a local historian."

"It seems rather of its time, and not very relevant to the modern world," sniffed Rambo, "I can't see there being any interest in reviving it."

"No, the principle Rambo, of locals showing off their baking skills. It could raise money for charity and bring people together as a community activity: a bit of fun."

"I thought you said it was to get people married?"

"Well in the old days I think that might have been part of the idea, but we wouldn't be approaching it from that angle. The revival would have a different emphasis, as I said."

"Even so, I think it is a silly idea," said Rambo.

"Oh, I thought the local historian would be keen to see it revived."

"Why," asked Rambo suspiciously.

"Because it would help drum up interest in Tangents' past, its curious ways and customs. Help create a demand perhaps for an author with a book on the subject."

"But my book has not been published."

"Precisely. And why not?"

"Because publishers are idiots."

"They are business people and they react to demand. They look at Tangents and say to themselves 'is there an interesting history to the village, are people clamouring to learn more about the history of this village?'"

"I don't think you've thought this through at all, Willoughby" said Rambo dismissively.

"How did it go with the police?" asked Willoughby.

"I was just telling Brian here, they were most unhelpful," replied Rambo indignantly.

Willoughby noticed that Brian was sunk deep in an armchair, with the crossword on the table in front of him. He also clocked that Brian was sound asleep.

"I didn't think they took me seriously."

"Really? Your story of a modern highwayman keeping watch on the roads of Tangents ready to pounce on any stray food?"

"Yes."

"What did they say to you?"

"They thanked me for making my report, but said there was nothing for them to go on, and said they had no intelligence of any food-stealing agents working in the area, nor of any highwaymen."

"How did they explain how your lunch vanished into thin air then?"

"They suggested it might have been foxes."

"I said that."

"It wasn't foxes," shouted Rambo. "Foxes don't use a knife and fork! People just don't take crime seriously, they never think it will happen to them so they are not on their guard and so get conned and stolen from. Not me though – I am guarding against it. There are so many scammers around, people telling stories which just aren't true."

"How are you going to stop people making up stories?"

"Well I can't stop people doing scams, but I can make sure I am not caught out by any. I sent off for a mail order book a few weeks ago entitled Your First Lesson In Being Scammed, which gives details of the type of scams and how to spot them so you don't get tricked."

"Is it good, the book?"

"Supposed to be very good, the advert had lots of quotes from people saying how invaluable it had been."

"Oh you haven't read it yet?"

"No."

"I think you've got to read it to get the full benefit, not just receive it."

"I haven't received it yet."

"Oh I thought you said you got it weeks ago."

"No," said Rambo, "I said I sent off for it weeks ago, I didn't say I had received it. But no doubt I will very soon. They have cashed my cheque a few weeks ago, so they obviously got my order."

"What else did the police say to you?"

"The police didn't tell me to get this book. That was done on my own initiative. No, the police were no help. They just advised me to keep my eyes open for anything unusual or suspicious."

"Did you tell them about the camel?"

"No, why would I?"

"Well isn't that unusual and suspicious: a wooden camel suddenly appearing in the car park and no one knows why?"

"Oh," said Rambo, "I hadn't thought about that. Do you think the two things could be connected – my lunch being stolen and this camel?"

"Well it would be a remarkable coincidence otherwise don't you think?"

"Yes, yes. But how could they be connected?"

"Well that's why we need the boys in blue to investigate, as they are trained in such matters. It could be anything.

Maybe it's a Trojan camel and the highwayman is hiding in there waiting for his moment to pounce? And where does the highwayman stash all his ill-gotten gains? He can't walk around Tangents with a big picnic hamper, that would look conspicuous. So perhaps he stashes it in the camel and comes back later to collect it. Perhaps there is a cool box inside it. Perhaps the whole thing is one big cool box. Or maybe there is a secret surveillance camera in it, feeding pictures back to him in his hideout. The possibilities are endless. Perhaps you should go back to the police and report a suspicious camel in the village and ask them to investigate? In fact, if I were you, I would go round there first thing tomorrow."

"They don't seem to take me seriously," lamented Rambo, "I doubt they'd come."

"Now, Rambo about this damn silly new card system."

"What?" said Rambo, not paying attention as he was thinking of what to do about the camel.

"This damn silly card system of yours – I can't get any food on it!"

"What, sorry?" said Rambo, who still was not listening.

"This silly card system – I can't get food on my card, only drink."

"Speak to the office about it, they'll sort that," said Rambo distractedly, "sorry must dash, I've got something important to do," and with that Rambo dashed off, leaving Willoughby's "No, hang on a minute..." hanging in the air.

Willoughby looked to see how Brian was doing with that day's crossword. There was only one clue left to do. Willoughby knew this would vex Brian, who always took pride in finishing the crossword. Willoughby looked up the relevant clue: 'Way to keep on time? (5,5)' and he looked at the skeleton: _ a _ c _ s _ r _ p.

After a few moments considering the clue, Willoughby quietly wrote in 'watch strap' in an almost exact copy of Brian's spidery handwriting, so that when Brian awoke he would see the finished crossword and presume that he must have finished it before he fell asleep.

Chapter 7

"Good morning padre," Willoughby greeted the vicar beside the 1st tee, "if indeed it is morning, not still the middle of the night."

"Yes, I must thank you all for being so obliging for starting at such an unusual hour to accommodate my diary. Sorry, did you manage to have breakfast?"

"Yes I forced down half a ramekin of sesame seeds garnished with two-fifths of a grape before I came out."

"Good, good," said the vicar, rummaging in his bag. Willoughby looked hopefully at what the vicar was doing, hoping he might provide some food, perhaps a cereal bar.

But it was a Sharpie pen which he then used to mark his ball with a red cross. "The others not arrived yet?" asked Willoughby.

"No, haven't seen Brian or Jerry. Oh, I dived deep into the old church records again after you had gone last night. I discovered some interesting things."

"Get to the bottom of the Taste of Tangents business?"

"I could not find any mentions of that anywhere. It occurred to me also after you'd gone that when your grandmother would have been coming of age the Great War was happening. I can't imagine the Taste of Tangents being held during the war when the young menfolk would have been away and anything that might strike as frivolity was frowned upon during that war. Also in the latter stages there was rationing which would surely have put paid to a food festival?"

"Ahhh. Well, perhaps it was my grandmother talking of something that had been told to her? I had just presumed that it was something she had participated in herself. Maybe she had been telling me something about what her parents' generation got up to. Maybe that was the root of her parents' union? Or maybe it was after the war? That might make a lot of sense if you think about it. If the generation of young males had been thinned out in Flanders Field then the young womenfolk would have a lot of competition for finding a husband? Perhaps this is the sad genesis of the festivities?"

"Possibly."

"Or maybe it was an old custom revived then from necessity? Mind you, a lot of these customs can be rooted in sad events like that Wife Carrying Championship." The vicar chuckled, but Willoughby ignored him. "That all started when the Viking raiders came and carried off the local womenfolk. Seems an odd thing to celebrate really your wife being kidnapped." Then he added on reflection: "Then again, perhaps not."

"Another thing I discovered," said the vicar, "is that, you know that patch of scruffy waste ground to the east of the village which used to have two rotting sheds on it?"

"Weren't they animal enclosures? Pigsties or something?"

"Well whatever they were, do you know who owns that land?"

"One of the pig's descendants? Rik-pig? That camel? Has he come to Tangents to claim his birthright?"

"It's the church. I noticed it last night in the records. We were bequeathed it – it was before my time – with the idea that it could be used as an overspill burial ground if one was needed. Well it never has been, nor ever will be now, with cremation now the norm."

"Oh you will have the property developers after you. They seem to be circling the village."

"I doubt it. I am not sure how useful that parcel of land would be for them – it's quite a small plot and I am not even sure how you would get access to it, certainly not with a car. I can't see it being an attractive proposition for a property developer. Oh good morning, Brian," he said, greeting the newcomer.

"Am I late?" asked Brian.

"Good morning," said Willoughby. "No, you're not late."

"Am I playing with you Willoughby?"

"No, I am playing with the padre."

"But you always partner him, I thought um this is the Bowler's Name competition when um we drew for partners? You know, so we get to play with different people."

"It is, Brian, but the padre drew me as partner."

"Am I playing with Harry? Doesn't he often play with you?"

"No, you drew George, Terry, er Jerry."

"Jerry Best? Oh I know him well."

"No, Harry is playing with some bod I don't know but apparently who he knows well."

"Sorry I am late," said Brian, "I have been speaking to the camel. Very clever isn't it?"

"You have been speaking to the camel?"

"Yes, we have just had a um conversation. We had um one last night too. Very clever, how does it do it? I thought it might just be a recording that was um activated by some sort of motion sensitive device when someone gets close, but it actually has a proper conversation with you. It calls you by your name."

"How did it know your name? Are you a well-known figure in wooden camel circles?" asked Willoughby.

"It asked me obviously."

"What did you two chat about?"

"Well when I was leaving the club last night, it was um quite late – I was the last to leave the clubhouse – and I was walking past the camel and it told me it wanted to get out."

"Get out of what? A parking ticket? Giving the speech at the next ladies' dinner?"

"Um, well the um car park I suppose."

"Maybe it wanted to feel sand under its feet," suggested Willoughby. "It is probably missing the desert. Did you move it into a bunker? There is room in the one on the 2nd now that the traction engine no longer uses it."

"Oh, no, I um could never move it on my own. I was sympathetic though, I said I was sure someone would come in the morning to move it. He said he didn't want moving, he wanted getting out. But I said there was nothing I could do at that time and I am sure someone would take him out in the morning. He said that was no damn good, he wanted letting out tonight and could I get someone."

"When I saw it this morning," Brian continued, "I asked it how it was and it said it wanted to get out. It asked me who I was, I told him and it said 'Brian get me out of here'. You go and have a chat with him," suggested Brian. "See if it will talk to you as well."

Willoughby went to see. "Good morning Mr Camel," he said, and then as an aside to Brian, "is it male do you think?" Then again he addressed the camel: "How are you this fine morning? Actually this rather horrible-looking morning."

"Who is that?" demanded the camel.

"See," said Brain, "told you."

"It's Willoughby."

"Oh thank goodness, I have just been speaking to that idiot Brian."

"He remembers you," remarked Willoughby to Brian, "that's nice."

"That's very clever, even remembering who it has spoken to. It's um so clever isn't it what they can do with technology," marvelled Brian.

"Can we help you with anything?" asked Willoughby.

"I want to get out!"

"It says that!" said Brian. "It doesn't have much by way of conversation does it, that's all it seems to say. Perhaps we should ask its name? What is your name?" said Brian slowly and carefully to the camel.

"Cyril Ramsbotham."

"It thinks it's Rambo!" said Brian. "Why on earth would it want to be Rambo?"

"I think rather it's the case that Rambo is inside it," suggested Willoughby.

"What, it has eaten Rambo?"

"More swallowed him whole," said Willoughby, "like Jonah and the whale."

"Can you get me out of here!" said Rambo.

"Er, how did you get in?"

"If you lift up the hump it opens."

Willoughby tried but failed, explaining, after some huffing and puffing, that: "It's jolly stiff, I can't open it."

"I know! That's why I am stuck here!" shouted Rambo. "If I could open the blasted thing I would have. It slammed shut when I was inside."

"Hallo, what's going on?" asked the just-arrived Jerry Best.

"The camel has swallowed Rambo whole," replied Brian, "and, um, perhaps Jonah and a whale, too."

"Oh, right," said Jerry. "What's going on Willoughby?"

"Brian's just told you – the camel has swallowed Rambo."

"Crikey has it? Is he all right?"

"Yes, the camel still looks fine," said Brian looking over it.

"I meant Rambo. Are you all right Rambo?" Jerry called out.

"No, of course I am not! I am stuck in this confounded thing. Can you get me out!"

"Here, Jerry, you are younger and stronger than us," said Willoughby, "can you help us pull open this trap door, it's as stiff as hell." The three of them pulled hard at it and finally prised it open. A rather aggrieved, bedraggled and looking-sorry-for-himself Rambo clambered out.

"How on earth did you get stuck in there?" asked Jerry.

"I had propped the door open, but the doorstop pinged out and trapped me."

"How long have you been in there?" asked Jerry.

"All flipping night. Some idiot came by last night and I told him I was stuck but they just said they were sure I would be let out in the morning and just left me in there."

"What were you doing in there in the first place Rambo?" asked Jerry.

"I was looking for Trojans, well not Trojans obviously, though I suppose they could be Trojans, but they wouldn't likely be Trojans would they in there, would they. Not here. I was looking for robbers or the highwaymen, well only one highwayman, well there could be more than one I suppose, or for stolen goods, or for surveillance equipment or for some clue as to what the camel was doing here and what it had to do with my lunch going missing."

"Did you find it?" asked Jerry.

"What?"

"Your lunch – was it in there?"

"I wasn't looking for my lunch!" shouted Rambo.

"No, it would have been your supper if it was last night," reasoned Brian.

"No, I wasn't looking for either my lunch or my supper in there. My lunch had been eaten!"

"You thought the camel had eaten your lunch?" asked Jerry.

"No of course not!" Rambo exploded. "That would be hardly flipping likely would it!"

"No. Camels only eat once every three months," Brian explained to Jerry.

"Plus this isn't a real camel, but one made out of wood," pointed out Willoughby to Brian.

"Also this isn't a real camel, but one made out of wood," Brian said to Jerry. "Oh, do you think perhaps this Jonah person ate your lunch?" Brian asked Rambo.

"Who on earth is Jonah?" Rambo demanded.

"I am not sure," said Brian, "but Willoughby knows him."

"I don't know him," said Willoughby. "Perhaps he is a new member?"

"I thought he had lunch here?" said Brian.

"Well not likely he's a member then if he can find lunch in this benighted place with this damn silly card system in operation. Now Rambo, about your blasted card system."

"Sorry Willoughby, can't stop here nattering. I've got to get home and have a bath and some breakfast."

"No, just hang on a minute..." said Willoughby, but Rambo was off.

"Rambo gets pottier doesn't he?" said Jerry with a certain amount of awe. "But we have a match to play and the forecast is horrendous: says there is storm brewing. So we better get on with it to see if we can get round in time."

But they did not.

The rain began while they were playing the 3rd hole, and by the 5th one it had become in Willoughby's words 'biblical rain' which he argued meant that the vicar was now in his comfort zone and so Willoughby explained that he was now confidently relying upon his partner to bring them home to victory. By the 7th hole puddles were beginning to form on the greens and on the 8th green Brian had no option but to putt through a puddle. The players had talked of abandoning the round there and then but Willoughby had persuaded them to carry on and play the 9th and take a view then and, if necessary, shelter underneath the halfway hut's verandah and see if the rain would ease.

Brian and Jerry won the 9th hole to level the match. Scanning the sky, the vicar said that it was clear that the rain was set in, and best to come back another day and complete the back nine, which all the others readily agreed to. The vicar headed back to the clubhouse and Brian went with him; but Jerry went with Willoughby to the halfway hut, Willoughby marching on eagerly ahead.

The halfway hut was closed. "Oh yes," said Jerry. "She wouldn't have opened up yet. We're still very early, I forgot. She wouldn't be expecting golfers at this hour. Won't be open for a while yet. Actually, I doubt she will open it today, not in this weather. No-one's going to be playing in this are they, and she'd get drenched herself coming here." Then he added: "Did you know the halfway hut comes under Greens Committee?"

"No," said a dejected Willoughby. "I'd have thought it'd be Estates, or maybe House."

"Apparently if it's on the golf course it's Greens, so I have the problem of it. I had no idea when I became Greens Chairman that I'd get landed with so much. I think the previous bod knew a thing or two when he resigned. He must have seen this all coming."

"I don't think anyone saw the problem with the 10th and 11th coming, thanks to Pike. Isn't that the problem?"

"Well the halfway hut was already in the Greens Committee's in-tray as it were."

"What's the issue there?"

"Well Mrs French has said she is keen to give it up. I think it has all got a bit much for her – she is, well, she must be in her seventies now and I think she lost a lot of enthusiasm for it when her sister moved away. I think it's become all a bit of a chore now, down here on her own, not helped that there is no proper access to this part of the course except by walking across the course, so she has to lug all the stuff down here on her own now – well she's taken to putting it all in a wheelbarrow and wheeling it down here," he laughed. "So we will need a new person to take over the halfway hut."

"Have you got someone else lined up?"

"No, haven't found anyone interested."

"I suppose you're not likely to in the current circs."

"But before that we'd probably need to do some work to it. It's beginning to show its age, and the cooking facilities need replacing."

"Is that your responsibility, I thought it was an outside business?"

"It is, but they pay us a sum to have the concession and as part of this the club has to provide the premises, so maintenance of the hut is our responsibility. The cooking equipment, I am hoping, is not. But I have yet to get that 100% confirmed. But if we are soon to lose this land, it isn't worth investing in the hut, and how will we get someone to take over if the halfway hut business has only a few months left? No-one is going to take that on. The club might have to step in and do something, or maybe we just abandon it."

"Would the club take it over?" asked Willoughby.

"Well only if the House Committee does."

"I thought you said the halfway hut is Greens?"

"The hut is, but if it's about catering then it's House."

"That would mean that silly card system coming here," cried Willoughby in alarm. "That would be a big mistake."

"What's wrong with the card system? An unnecessary flaff, I grant you, which seems more about Rambo wanting to wrest some control away from the Steward back to his committee than anything actually useful, but no harm to it surely?"

"No harm!" Willoughby exploded and told his tale of woe.

After this Jerry said: "I had wondered if we could just put a vending machine down here if we couldn't get anyone to man the hut. But turns out a vending machine would not come under Greens, so I can happily leave that to others."

"That would be House wouldn't it?"

"No, a vending machine in the halfway hut would be Estates. But the hut is the least of my problems at the moment. Got this pressing matter of the course. I hope my sudden calling of an emergency meeting struck people as dynamic and decisive rather than the blind panic of a newly installed Chairman of Greens?"

"No, it was generally much admired, I believe."

"Thank you Willoughby, most kind. But then you have always lied so beautifully."

"Anyone subsequently come up with any bright ideas?"

"No, but I have been wondering whether the eventual outcome should be that we go down to being a nine-hole course, sell off some of the extra land ourselves for housing, which would put us on a sounder financial footing. Then we'd have to decide where to keep nine existing holes or whether we could redesign the whole plot of land and try to build a really top-class nine holer."

"I had been wondering that, too," said Willoughby. "Trouble is there is such snobbery about nine holers. Look at all those top-100 course lists – you never see a nine-hole course get into them, even ones with a different set of tees on the back nine. Even Royal Worlington no longer seems to sneak in at number 100."

"Daft isn't it," agreed Jerry. "I'd much rather play a really good nine-hole course than an average 18-hole one. But others don't see it that way. So I can't see that making this a nine-hole course would go down well and if we just use nine of the existing holes – well there isn't an obvious routing which would include all the best ones is there. If we rip it all up and start again from scratch, can we find a way to play golf here in the meantime? Do we have to close the course for a while? Or can we weave a six or nine-hole hole layout using temporary tees and greens with several short holes? Either way, there'll be a hiatus for a while – for a year or two, maybe even longer. Will we hang on to all our members through this period?"

"I thought we'd decided we'll go for the land at Winnie's Place and build two new holes there?"

"Well, we haven't got that land yet have we and then there's the cost of knocking down the house and building the holes. Can we afford it? If we can, well I was looking at the plot and it will take some imagination to turn a couple of good holes out of that, or even one good hole and one mediocre one. I am not sure that is necessarily the solution to our problems."

"I'm not so sure," said Willoughby. "Keep pushing that option would be my advice."

"Rain seems to be easing a tad. Shall we head back?" suggested Jerry. "Tell you what, I'll treat you to a sausage sandwich in the clubhouse so long as we don't drown on the way back."

"You're on!" said Willoughby enthusiastically.

"Can I order two sausage sandwiches please Steward," commanded Willoughby when he got back to the clubhouse.

"Have you sorted out the problem with your card, Sir?" replied the Steward.

"No, Jerry Best is buying these. On his card. Oh that's a point, he wanted a sausage sandwich, too. Make that three sausage sandwiches please Steward."

"Do you have his card?"

"Er, no."

"I will need his card to process the order, Sir."

"Oh this damn silly card system. He'll be along soon, he is in the locker room making himself look less like a drowned rat. Can't you just tell the kitchen to fire up the grill and Jerry'll be along in a moment to do the admin?"

"No, Sir."

"Ah, here is Jerry anyway. Or a partially drowned rat – tricky to tell from this distance. Either way I'd advise us both to make sure we do not get bitten by him."

"Two sausage sandwiches please Steward," said Jerry. "Or have you already ordered, Willoughby?"

"No," replied Willoughby.

"Sorry, Sir, may I ask you to make it clear exactly what you wish to order? Is the order for two sausage sandwiches; or is it for three sausage sandwiches; or is it for five sausage sandwiches?"

"Why would I be ordering five sandwiches?" said Jerry.

"Mr Cornwallis has already tried to order three sausage sandwiches on your behalf."

"Three?" said Jerry looking at Willoughby.

"One was for you," explained Willoughby. "You said you'd have one, too."

"Can I have two sausage sandwiches please Steward," said Jerry.

"Is that two sausages sandwiches for you, Sir, and two for Mr Cornwallis, so for four sausage sandwiches?"

"No. It's for one each, so a sum total of two. Can I place a total order of two sausage sandwiches."

"No, Sir."

"Oh, is the kitchen already doing three sandwiches? That's fine – three sausage sandwiches then."

"Sorry Sir, you cannot have three sausage sandwiches."

"Well how many sausage sandwiches can I have then?" said Jerry, failing to keep a note of exasperation out of his voice.

"None, Sir. The kitchen is not open yet."

"Oh heck – I keep forgetting how early it is," said Jerry. "Comes from teeing off in the middle of the night. Sorry Willoughby about the sandwiches. Well I'm off to plunge into a hot bath. See you tomorrow on the 10th tee, and we'll resume all square."

"So you haven't managed to sort out your card, Sir?" the Steward asked Willoughby.

"No."

"I can offer you a packet of cheese-and-onion crisps."

"Thank you. But no."

"It would be on the house, Sir."

"Don't happen to like crisps. Of all the wonderful things that can be done with potatoes – gratin, scalloped, maluns Bombay, rosti, boxty, dum aloo, fondant, knish, dauphine crocchè, Lyonnaise, truffade, Pommes Jenna, Pommes sufflées, Pommes sarladaise – or even just the humble mash, turning them into crisps seems a crime. Cheese and onion? I thought you had got rid of the last of those. I thought Rik-pig had been doing the club sterling service by chomping his way through boxes and boxes of our cheese-and-onion crisps. For which he should have been awarded at least honorary membership, and probably made an honorary vice president of the club – though, come to think of it, Brian did indeed once propose in committee that he could be made a member – but instead the poor soul is carted off to market."

"Yes, I was aware of the pig's imminent demise. Mr King informed me of it."

"Perhaps the committee should attend its funeral to make sure it is sent off with full honours. Maybe the committee could line up outside the abattoir and the pig's carcass be processed out through an arch of mashie niblicks."

"I believe the sword arch is more customary for weddings than funerals, Sir."

"Some marriages are a lot like funerals. Anyway, why are you still hawking cheese-and-onion crisps? I thought the club was finally a cheese-and-onion crisp free zone."

"It was, Sir, for a brief period yesterday afternoon, after Mr King had collected the last box of crisps. Then several more boxes of cheese-and-onion crisps were delivered to the club."

"How come?"

"It is this new card system. It automatically works out what is popular and reorders it."

"But the crisps weren't popular. Harry is not sure even how much the poor pig liked them."

"But the computer registered that a large amount of crisps were passing through the system, so decided that they were popular and automatically reordered some more. Several boxes more."

"Oh dear."

"I was hoping to revive the trade with Paddock's Farm, but I understand the pig is not being replaced."

"Yes, it's always been Rikki's pig and now she is away at uni the line of pigs is about to drift to an end. Don't fancy becoming a pig farmer yourself? The vicar can offer you some land with some second-hand pigsties on them which an estate agent would describe as having experienced deferred maintenance thereby providing a perfect opportunity for a new owner to put their own stamp on the place."

"No, Sir."

"Quite sure?"

"Yes, Sir."

"Well I have another idea how you could shift some of your new crisp mountain. But it would involve you doing me a favour in return…"

Chapter 8

"Oh hallo Jerry, you're prompt," said Willoughby as he approached the 10th tee in readiness for the resumption of the Bowler's Name match, "been getting some practice in?"

"No, just had to do a bit of business. Anyway there is nowhere to properly practice at this club. That's one of the drawbacks of this place."

"Oh hallo Brian," said Willoughby, greeting the new arrival. "I should complain to the Chairman of Greens," said Willoughby to Jerry, "about the lack of practice facilities. I hear there's a new dynamic chap in post."

"What should I complain about?" asked Brian.

"No, not you Brian. Jerry. About the lack of practice facilities at the club."

"Oh, um I see. Yes it would be good if we have a practice putting green or something, or just a net. Why don't you write it as a suggestion in the club's suggestions book," suggested Brian to Jerry.

"I didn't even know we had a suggestions book," replied Jerry.

"Um, no we don't actually," said Brian. "Better put down another suggestion that we should have a suggestions book."

"But how could I make that suggestion?"

"Well um put that one in the suggestion book, too, I suppose."

"No room sadly," said Jerry returning to Willoughby's point about practice facilities. "Even a small practice putting green isn't possible. Well not anywhere by the 1st tee anyway. But I was thinking about that last night: maybe if we do drop down to nine holes, with some of the extra land we could give ourselves a driving range and practice putting green. Rescue something from the embers.”

As Jerry had been talking, Willoughby had unzipped his golf bag and brought out a plastic container. “What’s that for?” asked Jerry.

“Well last night I was thinking ‘what about a little something’ and me replying ‘well I shouldn’t mind a little something’, and of course there wasn’t even the littlest something to be had. So I thought I would stock up with some essential supplies while I am here, to ward off the night starvation. Well the day starvation as well, now.”

“Sorry the halfway hut is closed: Mrs French is ill.”

“Oh, that’s terrible. Terrible.”

“Oh don’t worry, it’s nothing serious. She has just gone down with a cold. She got caught in yesterday’s downpour. She’s just nursing herself and ensuring she keeps warm and inside for a few days, or a week or so.”

“That’s terrible news,” said Willoughby.

“Don’t worry, she’s not seriously ill – it’s merely a cold as I said. That’s what I was doing – taking down the closed for funeral sign and putting up a closed due to illness sign.”

“A week,” said Willoughby disconsolately, lost in his own thoughts.

“I think she might be making a meal of it,” said Jerry.

“Sorry, did you say she’s making a meal?” asked Willoughby perking up.

“Making a meal of this cold, I said. But I couldn’t really say anything especially as it’s her business anyway, not the club’s, so it is entirely up to her whether she opens or not. As I was saying yesterday, I think her enthusiasm for the hut has waned. Ah, here comes the vicar: we have a quorum. Better get going as there’s someone coming down the 9th. It’s our honour isn’t it?”

After the vicar had missed an eminently sinkable putt on the 18th, the third time he had missed one of those in those nine holes, to give Brian and Jerry a 1-up victory, and the vicar had shot off to take a confirmation class, and Jerry to do some work, Willoughby made his way to the clubhouse. He ordered himself a drink and waited for Brian to join him.

Martin Cowmeadow walked in. "Ah Willoughby I had a word just now with the Chairman of General Purposes about the honours board. He says it isn't up to them, reckons it would be a Finance Committee matter. Sorry, I know you were going to ask him, but as I was helping him get Rambo out of the camel it seemed an opportune moment to ask."

"He'd gone back in there had he?"

"What do you mean 'gone back in'?"

"Brian got him out; well Brian, George and I in fact fished him out yesterday morning. Rambo had spent the night in there."

"Why?"

"Goodness knows. Perhaps he just fancied a sleep and maybe thought why not pop in to the camel for some shut eye, save the effort of walking all the way home and clambering into a warm, comfortable bed. What was he doing in the camel? Had he spent another night in it?"

"Don't think so. Wasn't really clear why he was in there, but it was something about a torch."

"Maybe he felt like an afternoon nap and popped in there to have 40 winks."

"Why would that involve a torch?"

"Maybe he is scared of the dark, and so has to sleep with a light on?"

"Well, must dash. Shall you have a word with the Chairman of Finance or shall I?"

"I will – and thanks for asking the General Purposes bod." As Martin left he passed Brian entering.

"Well, well played Brian," said Willoughby, "can I buy you a drink to celebrate your victory? What would you like?"

"Would it be your usual Sir?" asked the Steward of Brian.

"Is that, um, what I normally have?" asked Brian.

"Yes, Sir."

"Well um yes please then," said Brian ambling over to an armchair, almost colliding with a rapidly entering Rambo as he did so. Rambo, looking round the room, asked "Is Harry here?"

"Is Harry Here what?" asked Brian.

"Is Harry here in the clubhouse?"

"Oh I don't actually know him. But he's thinking of becoming a member I'm told."

"Oh course you do!" said Rambo impatiently. "He's a friend of Willoughby's."

"Oh you can ask Willoughby then – he's at the bar."

When Willoughby came back with the drinks Brian said: "Rambo is looking for a friend of yours, a Mr Here."

"Harry! I was looking for Harry!"

"Harry? Oh, you mean Larry; no hang on, he is called Harry isn't he. Very confusing the way he keeps changing his name. He's gone to the station to collect Rikki. I hear you have been eaten by the camel again, Rambo."

"I was not eaten."

"No, more swallowed whole. I think you ought to be more careful around it: it seems to be short-sighted as it seems to keep confusing you with an oyster. Or maybe just act less like an oyster when you are around it?"

"I was looking for my torch!" said Rambo indignantly.

"It had swallowed your torch had it? What an eclectic taste in foodstuffs it has."

"No, it had not swallowed my torch. I had left it in there."

"For when you returned for a zizz?"

"No by accident last time. There is nothing in there you know, Willoughby. The camel. It is empty. You were saying you thought there would be cameras in there or a cold box, but there is nothing."

"Do you remember the story of the wooden horse?"

"You mean the Trojan horse."

"No the wooden horse, the vaulting horse some British prisoners of war used to tunnel out of a POW camp. They built a wooden horse to hide the tunnellers in and to cart the dug-out earth away. Well they didn't start tunnelling at first, as they knew the guards would be suspicious, and would check out the horse when it was put away etc. Only when the guards' suspicions were allayed did they kit out the horse for tunnelling. Do you think your highwayman may be doing the same? Lulling you into a false sense of security? Perhaps he is waiting until you, who is the only person apparently clever enough to have sussed his devious plan, has convinced yourself there is nothing in it?"

"Well perhaps," said Rambo. "Do you think so?"

"Well I am not expert in crime detection. I am well out of my depth here. You need old whatshisname, oh no, that's no good, he's retired now and is busy beekeeping in the South Downs, so he wouldn't take your case. Perhaps you should go back to the police and explain exactly what is going on? They are the experts. I regret that I am at a loss. But then it is a capital mistake to theorise before one has data. All you have discovered is that the highwayman, if indeed this is his work, has not yet equipped the camel. You do not know when he will do so, or indeed if he ever will do so. Perhaps the camel is merely a decoy – maybe he wants everyone to be so focused on the camel that he can use his real hideout elsewhere with no fear of discovery? These are very deep waters, but pray go on with your narrative."

"But I don't think the police took me seriously when I went in last time."

"You may have just caught them at the wrong moment. They had probably just put the kettle on and were looking forward to putting their feet up and tackling the crossword with a refreshing brew and a biccy and in walks you and so they missed their elevenses. I would go back and see them if I were you. But not at 11 o'clock. Maybe not at 4 o'clock either. You have a duty to ensure Tangents' safety knowing what you have discovered. Sounds like this highwayman is playing the long game. If there is a highwayman – I still believe it was probably foxes who wolfed your lunch."

"It was not foxes! Foxes do not use a knife and fork!"

"Refined foxes might?"

"That is typical of a lax attitude to crime, if you don't mind me saying so, Willoughby, which threatens our village. I have arranged for a talk in the clubhouse to tackle this. It's by some retired detectives about preventing burglary. People are very complacent about crime and con tricks. They always think it won't happen to them. Oh yes, Willoughby, I meant to say, I have been researching the Taste of Tangents," Rambo continued, "I have discovered something that I bet you didn't know."

"Have you?"

"Yes and I bet you didn't know it."

"Well you are the local historian Rambo. I am sure there are lots of things you have researched I don't know about, albeit not as many one may have hoped, as you have told me about lots of them in excessive and repetitive detail."

"Yes," said Rambo, "there was a speciality section to the Taste of Tangents."

"Was there? No, I can honestly say my Grandmother never told me about that. What, pray, is one of those?"

"Well it all started when there was a glut of apples locally in the village, a bumper harvest from some orchards that used to be here, and as a way to find some imaginative ways to use apples, that year's Taste of Tangents had a Speciality Section whereby the cooks had to make something with apples. I was thinking if you wanted to make your revival of a Taste of Tangents authentic you should include this."

"What with items made using apples?"

"Well it doesn't have to be apples. If you revive it, you should do something different. I was thinking crisps."

"Crisps?"

"Yes, crisps."

"You don't make things with crisps."

"Yes you can. They are ingredients in many things. It would be an excellent way to showcase people's originality. There are lots of recipes that involve crisps. I think that would capture people's imaginations, rather than your silly idea of it being a marriage bureau. My idea is that it would be a showcase of people's cooking skills. Having researched it properly, unlike you, I have discovered this and I think we should go ahead with a revival of the Taste of Tangents. As you correctly said, it is important to honour our history. Just in a sensible way, not in the way you intended. I have got some crisps in readiness. Please tell all entrants to come here and get their crisps for the Taste of Tangents. We could set up the registration here. Be a way of the club carrying out its policy of integrating itself with the local community, I bet you hadn't thought of that aspect either Willoughby. Good job you got me involved."

"Oh talking about the matter of food Rambo – this damn silly card system."

"Sorry Willoughby, can't hang around here. Got things to do – must dash!" and with that Rambo shot off.

Whilst Rambo was being hauled out of the camel Harry had been collecting Rikki at the train station. He had been slightly disappointed that the first question Rikki had asked about anyone was not of Harry and how he was but how was Willoughby and had Harry been making sure that he wasn't getting into mischief. But he was pleased, as they bowled along the country lanes, that the conversation had now turned to Rik-pig. "I have noticed some odd habits he has," Harry was saying. "Don't know what they mean, if anything. But he tends to come up to me and nuzzle me and huff and blow air on me. Not sure why, but he does."

"Oh that's a way pigs show affection for someone."

"Is it? Oh I didn't know that. I had also noticed he tends to wag his tail when I am there, and I know dogs do that when they are happy, but I don't know about pigs."

"Pigs are just the same – if they wag their tails that shows they are happy."

"Oh good – he does that a lot when I am around."

"Hang on, what's this?" Rikki interrupted him. "Someone in trouble. Someone broken down?"

A figure in black was flagging them down. "Maybe it's a highwayman," Rikki laughed.

Chapter 9

As Harry slowed the car to a standstill, he and Rikki were able to make out the figure in the black cape more clearly. The person who was standing in the middle of the lane holding up a hand imperiously to them was someone they recognised.

Harry wound down his window: "You in a spot of trouble Rambo? Can we help? Car broken down? Or won't start?" Harry asked, then wondered why, if so, Rambo had not just gone into the clubhouse to seek help. Maybe he had, but no-one had the jump leads he needed. "I have jump leads in the back if you need them."

"I thought that was your car Harry," Rambo replied, if replied is the right word when the other person has not listened to what had just been said to them. "I have a good eye for that sort of thing. I wanted to ask if you were okay. Are you okay Harry?"

"Er, yes, I'm fine, thanks. Er, how are you?"

"Oh good, good. I'll make sure that highwayman does not get you. Don't you worry."

"Oh, er, thank you," said Harry. "Well I'd better not stay here blocking the lane."

"Well I can't stand here talking either," said Rambo huffily. "I have got to see the vicar on an important piece of business. I am reviving an old Tangents tradition. It is part of my important work as the local historian."

"Well that was nice of him," remarked Harry to Rikki as they pulled away.

"Was it?"

"Yes, promising to save me from highwaymen. A kind gesture, I thought."

"Just struck me as odd."

"Why, you'd prefer me to be got by highwaymen?"

"No, I mean why does he think that highwaymen are operating here?"

"Goodness knows. He gets pottier by the day. He had to be helped out of the camel the other morning after he had spent the night in there."

"He was in a camel?"

"Not a real camel, obviously. A wooden one. A large wooden camel has appeared in the golf club car park."

"Why?"

"No one seems to know."

"Have you asked Willoughby? I imagine he is involved in it in some way; he does like to get up to mischief. I had told you to keep an eye on him and stop him getting into mischief," Rikki chided him.

"He doesn't know what the camel is doing there either. No one does."

"Are you sure? He does fib so."

"No, I believe he genuinely doesn't know. But I am being blamed for it. The camel I mean."

"Why?"

"The Secretary is telling people I put it there."

"Why?"

"I'm not entirely sure. He's an odd soul isn't he, the Secretary. Well here we are: home again, home again, jiggety-jig as my mother would say when we returned from somewhere."

"Why?"

"It is the kind of thing you just take for granted when you are little. Only after someone has gone do you wonder why. But I looked it up, it's part of an old nursery rhyme:

> *To market, to market, to buy a fat pig,*
> *Home again, home again, jiggety-jig.*

> *To market, to market, to buy a fat hog,*
> *Home again, home again, jiggety-jog.*

Oh by the way, I have arranged for us all to meet Willoughby this evening at the club for a drink. Hope that's okay?"

"That's splendid. Should I tell him that a rhyme about a fat pig seems to have reminded you of Willoughby?"

"Oh, no. Oh dear, no. Mind you, his wife does have him on a diet."

"Has she? Bet he's not happy!"

"No, he is feeling monumentally sorry for himself."

"Is he looking slimmer?"

"Not really."

While Harry was carrying Rikki's bag from the car into the house, Rambo had cornered the vicar in the church. "Ah Reverend Smith, I was hoping I would find you here. I wish to talk to you about the Taste of Tangents that you are organising."

"Not me, no."

"Oh, I thought you were involved?"

"Involved, yes; organising, no."

"I wanted to talk to you about the Speciality Section."

"I am afraid that I am not allowed to talk to anyone about the Taste of Tangents. The vicar has to remain impartial and above it all. That is the tradition as I am sure you know as our esteemed local historian. Just as, I am sure you know, I am forbidden by the long-established traditions of the event from talking to anyone about the event. You would need to speak to the Taster. He does all that side of things."

"Who is the Taster?"

"Willoughby Cornwallis, I believe."

"Oh, I have been talking to him about the Speciality –"

"Ah, ahh, ah," said the vicar, holding up a hand in warning. "You can't tell or ask me anything, remember. We have to respect our village history."

"Oh. I was just going to say that it was a way to integrate the golf club with the local community, which we on the Heads Of Committee, of which I am the Chairman, are always looking to do. Another thing I am doing to help the local community is put on a talk at the golf club about how to prevent burglaries, by some retired policeman. I think I should make it the first in a two-part lecture series. The other would be on scams."

"They also give talks on these?"

"No, that talk would be by me. I have a book on how to avoid scams, which I intend to use as the basis of a talk by me."

"Is it a good book then?"

"I haven't got it yet. I ordered it ages ago so it should come very soon. It's had good reviews – the advert said so. So I am sure it will be useful to me in writing my talk."

"I am not sure the village will have the appetite for two talks on crime. Perhaps wisest just to stick to the one?"

"People are so complacent about crime, they never think it will happen to them. But it can strike anytime: people need to be more vigilant."

"Is Tangents a hotbed of crime then? I had not noticed."

"There was my lunch, which was left outside my writing hut which someone stole and ate."

"Oh I heard about that. Sounded to me it was the work of foxes, they can be terribly bold at times. I remember –"

"It was not foxes!" Rambo cut off the vicar. "Foxes do not use a knife and fork! It was not foxes!"

Chapter 10

"Ah, Half Pint," Willoughby cried delightedly as Rikki entered the bar of the clubhouse. "Jolly good to see you. Fancy a snifter?"

"Why ever not. Gin and tonic please. Very kind."

"Been sent down from uni have you? Got the Dean's son in trouble? Got busted for smoking behind the bike sheds? Or have the dons sent you down for always telling them off and contradicting them?"

"I do not contradict people and tell them off!"

"Yes you do."

"No I don't! Behave yourself Willoughby."

"You're doing it yet again. Hah – got you there!"

"I am down here for a family conference. To discuss business relating to Paddock's Farm. As I am sure you know full well, and you are just being mischievous."

"Ah Steward," said Willoughby. "Can I have a gin and tonic please for Half Pint here, and better slosh some more into my glass as the tide seems to have gone out."

"Yes, Sir, and this will be on which account?"

"On mine: Willoughby Cornwallis."

"Very good, Sir."

"Yes, Anun was telling me your mother had had an offer for part of your lands."

"In some ways it is an attractive proposition. Mumsie can't cope with it all so easily nowadays and it's never been exactly a gold mine at the best of times, and this would be a way of bringing in money and reducing the acreage needing looking after. So it sort of makes sense."

"You don't sound that keen on it?"

"No, well I'm not. I can see the business rationale. But well, it's the home I grew up in, it would be a shame to see it broken up like that. Well for intrusive housing anyway. The view from the farm would not be of our fields and across to the golf course in the distance but of houses blocking our view."

"Would they?"

"Yes the property developer is only interested in having the best views, which means in turn we won't get them. Could be a bit, well, claustrophobic for us I fear; in comparison with what we have been used to anyway. He has done some mock ups of what it could look like and, well they are not attractive houses. Well, to my mind anyway. I suppose it may depend upon your taste. But not in keeping with the village certainly."

"Will the developer get planning permission?"

"Felix... oh you don't know Felix do you?"

"Anun's latest beau? Yes, I have spoken to him. Property lawyer."

"That's the chap. He says that he would. The access is there and it would not impinge on anyone bar possibly us and we couldn't object as that would be part of the deal."

"Anun told me a bit about it. She didn't seem keen."

"She isn't. She'd prefer an income stream over a sale of assets. But how do we get that from the land? That is what Mumsie has been trying to do all these years, to get a decent income out of it and well it wasn't easy then, and now Mumsie cannot get around so well and if Anun and I are not here she's short-staffed as it were unless she pays someone and paying someone may create more cashflow problems than it solves. Maybe it is for the best; or for the least worst anyway."

"What does your mother feel?"

"Well she won't welcome housing on her land. Well, what used to have been her land it'd be then. But, well, as I said it might be the least worst option. I think she is hoping that barn can be turned into an income stream somehow – B&B accommodation, holiday lets, something in that line.”

"Would you not want to stay on the farm after uni?”

"Well I've got to make a living then, and I don't think the farm will support Mumsie and I in the manner to which we would like to become accustomed. So, even if I stay here, I'd have to work elsewhere to earn money so that still leaves Mumsie a farmhand short. Anun does her bit cheerfully enough, but she is not that into farm life so she will be off to the bright city lights and a life as a career girl and a world of little black dresses. She'll be good at it, too.”

"But you are more a country gal?”

"Well I do like waking up each morning on a farm. I don't think I'd like to wake up every morning in a cityscape. But let's talk of something else. I have just had lots of this and it all a bit gloomsterish. How was your golf? I hear you had a match today. Harry won his yesterday. Did you win yours?”

"I was mildly magnificent in it.”

"But did you win?”

"I was playing with the vicar, who was also magnificent but in a much milder way. So we lost. He had his usual problem putting.”

"Hey, I was going to ask, what's this about highwaymen?”

"Rambo thinks that there is a highwayman operating in the village.”

"Why?”

"When you look at these scattered houses, you are impressed by their beauty. He looks at them, and the only thought which comes to him is a feeling of their isolation and of the impunity with which crime may be committed here.”

"Good heavens, cry I!" responded Rikki. "Who would associate crime with our dear old homesteads?"

"Rambo, it seems. Some foxes ate his lunch and he is convinced that it is the work of a highwayman."

"We got flagged down by this figure dressed in a black cape when we were driving back from the station. He was standing in the middle of the road holding us up."

"So there is a highwayman? Well I never. So Rambo was right."

"It was Rambo."

"You mean he was the highwayman? You saw through his disguise?"

"No, there was no disguise, he was in that tatty black cape he often wears and looking, well, exactly like Rambo."

"No face mask, no wild rag pulled up over his nose and mouth to disguise his features?"

"No."

"Well he is not going to be successful as a highwayman if he can't even be bothered with a rudimentary disguise. Did he steal your jewels?"

"No, he just said he'd protect Harry from the highwayman and then buzzed off."

"But if he is the highwayman, surely all he is doing is offering to protect you from himself? Sounds like he is operating a protection racket. Oh dear, maybe the isolated homesteads of Tangents are attracting the criminal fraternity: first Benton and now Rambo. But from the sound of it, Rambo will get caught jolly soon. He seems a highly incompetent criminal. But I imagine he will cope with prison well enough what with his wife shutting him in her garden shed all day."

"This highwayman business has nothing to do with you?"

"You have seen for yourself it is not. It is Rambo who is

putting round this story and now you tell me it is Rambo who is also the highwayman. Did he have any foxes with him when he did your hold up?"

"No!"

"Seems like he is acting alone. I had wondered if the foxes were in on it. Maybe they fell out over them eating his lunch. Mind you, they still could be the brains behind it as Rambo is hardly likely to be the brains behind anything."

"Oh Willoughby you do fib so! I have missed you. Have you missed me?"

"If I had a flower for every time I thought of you I could walk through my garden forever. Well my window box; well plant out a flower pot. A small one, anyway. Probably. Perhaps."

"Well I have thought of you. I have been wondering what mischief you have been up to while I have been away. I told Harry to keep an eye out for your doings, but as far I can gather he has been spending all his time writing and spending time with Rik-pig."

"Yes, he has been teaching it the offside law."

"What's that?"

"A thing in football, which females famously struggle to understand. And pigs, too, I have learned. So a sow presumably would have absolutely no chance."

"Oh, that is what a football was doing in there. I had wondered. So he didn't succeed?"

"Don't blame Harry. It appears the pig is simply not an association football man. Harry says he snuffled a bit at the football and wondered whether to take a bite of it and then ignored it. I think Harry was hoping he could have a kickaround with it, as a way of passing the time between Rik-pig having his sty doused in cheese-and-onion crisps. Maybe he is more of a rugger man, er rugger pig. That may be more his line, as when we played rugger at school it involved lots of rolling about in the mud, especially games on Lower Side where the pitch drained abominably, and pigs go in for that sort of thing I am told. Mind you, you can't play rugger on your own. Perhaps Harry should try him at golf? Does your mother still have that painting of a pig playing golf, maybe you could hang it in his sty to give him inspiration and help brighten the place up a bit?"

"I hope Harry won't miss having a pig too much," said Rikki. "He has grown so fond of Rik-pig."

"I am pretty sure he will be big and brave about it," Willoughby reassured her.

"Are you quite sure that you haven't been getting up to mischief?"

"I am as pure as the driven snow, as always. In fact, as I told Harry and he can testify, I went out the other day in the snow and people kept bumping into me as they didn't even see me there. I showed Harry my bruises. He said they looked deeply painful and was impressed how I didn't make a fuss, despite these horrific wounds, but acted like a brave little soldier."

"Little?"

"Yes, little. Have you not noticed how I am but a shadow of a man; indeed shadows of men are more voluminous than I. When I go out with Mrs C on windy days now she has to put me on a lead as otherwise I get blown away. As it is, people ask her why she is flying a kite."

"So if you haven't been getting up to mischief, then what have you been doing?"

"I have become involved as Godfrey Flower's executor. His cousin was doing it all, but she needs some help and I was already named in the will as responsible for some of the distribution, so I have been helping her. It's odd how you learn a lot about people in death that you don't know about when they were alive. Take Godders: I never knew half of what he did in his life, I now realise. I really wish I had. Really interesting, some of it. Turns out he was a great one for supporting enterprises he believed in, start-up firms he liked the sound of, or where he knew the people. He was a reasonably wealthy man with no family of his own and fairly modest tastes so I suppose it was a way to put his money to some good and help others.

"But he was also a would-be entrepreneur on the sly," Willoughby continued. "Turns out he owns, owned, some parcels of land which apparently he once thought of developing, but never did. He even owned shares in a gold mine," Willoughby laughed at this, "well a firm prospecting for gold would be more accurate. I don't think they ever struck gold, well not yet anyway, and so neither did Godders. All been a bit complicated as sometimes he had bought shares in the enterprise, sometimes it was a loan, sometimes seed money, and we are having to unpick it all. No doubt it all made sense to Godders and he knew what he was doing, but it has not always been easy for his cousin and I to sort it all out, and some of the money raised from the sale of some assets are ear-marked for certain things, so we have to keep track of it all. That has, in your words, been keeping me out of mischief. Not that I ever get into mischief anyway."

"He was your good friend wasn't he?" said Rikki gently.

"Yes. Knew him man and boy. If you look at that honours board," he said pointing, "you see our names entwined, as two-time winners of the Junior Foursomes. Oh that reminds me, I must see old whatshisname about getting that new honours board approved for Harry's competition." Then after a pause, he said: "Well, perhaps only partially knew him. Sterling fellow, and his sterlingness has been ever more apparent than after he's gone. Wish I'd known this about him. A great believer in Tangents, too, that has become clear. But then he lived here man and boy; never went away. Well except for university."

"Hey, have I told you about my friend Raine at uni?"

"A rather wet individual I believe."

"No she is not! Why do you say that! She is very jolly and go getting. Did I tell you there is a golf course in St Andrews?"

"No, but I was aware there was one."

"Were you?"

"Yes, it's quite well known."

"Is it? Well Raine has joined the Ladies Punting Club."

"Where on earth can you go punting in St Andrews?"

"On the punting green. Every week they have a punting competition and I go along some weeks as they are a very jolly crowd."

"Do you mean putting?"

"Punting – when you punt the ball along the ground trying to get it in those little holes. And when you do, you fish it out and find another hole and try to punt it into that instead."

"You mean putting. You're at the wrong university for punting. We did that at Cambridge, punting along the river in the summer. I was a member of a punting club. We would load our punt up with picnic things and then we'd punt along the river and choose a suitable spot and unload all the picnic things and have a picnic, and then we'd load all the clobber back on the punt and come back and then unload it again when we got back. Then it was decided it would be easier rather than load the picnic stuff onto the punt, and then unload it, and then load it back on again and then off again, just to have a picnic on the riverbank."

"I thought it was punting. Is it really called putting?"

"Yes, dafty."

"Well how was I to know? You have all sorts of silly names in golf, like the name you golfers give sandpits. It's all bonkers."

"Not bonkers: bunkers. Have you had a hearing test recently Half Pint? I think you may need one."

"Pardon?"

"I said –"

"Hah! Got you there! One-all."

"It was not a fair fight, you are taking advantage of my weakened state. I have not eaten for weeks. It dulls the mental facilities. As Elliott George so sensibly pointed out, no man can be wise on an empty stomach. What, you are actually playing golf Half Pint? Have you had a bang on the head or something? Or am I hallucinating due to a severe lack of food?"

"No, of course not. Afterwards they have cocoa and buns and I go along and join them in that. But Raine is getting quite into golf from her punting competitions. She says punting, er putting you say – are you sure it's putting?"

"Yes, ask anyone. Punting is what you do in boats along rivers, or in rugger matches for that matter as a way to avoid some ten-ton thug squashing you into the mud."

"How can you have a boat in a rugby match? Now you are just teasing me. Oh, you do fib so. Raine says it's a really good way to get into golf as she says it's much easier than all the rest of it. Plus of course it gets it over with quicker so you can have your cocoa earlier and don't have to walk all over the shop lugging a heavy bag and looking in bushes for where that silly little ball has gone."

"The others will be coming along soon," continued Rikki, "they are just finishing some more work to the conversion. I feel sorry for Harry's cousin, I thought he was coming here for a bit of a break and instead he seems to spend all the time working. It's turning into a busman's holiday for him. Perhaps you could invite him out for a game of golf? He can't play with Harry because he has to borrow Harry's clubs to play, and apparently every golfer has to have their own set of clubs as they won't play nice and share."

"I have played with him, and tell him I would happily do so again."

"Oh, isn't he very good?"

"That is not the reason! But no he is not. He tries to catch the hole unawares by lulling it into a false sense of security. He zig zags down the fairways as though he had no fixed purpose or aim in mind, and when the green relaxes and thinks it won't have yet another a hard object hitting it and causing bruising – like all those people did to me in the snow – he fires in a shot straight at it. Catches it totally off guard. Most entertaining tactic. Not one I would advise myself to the apprentice golfer as your friend Raine, but Marmaduke is clearly a chap who favours deception."

"Ah here they are!" said Rikki, spying Anun and Harry coming through the door.

"I saw your good lady wife earlier – and indeed just now," said Anun to Willoughby.

"I am no bigamist. I have but one wife."

"It was to her I was referring."

"Oh." said Willoughby, then, suddenly seized with panic: "She's not coming here is she?"

"It would be hard to give a definitive direction to her travels as she was tacking this way and that –"

"That would be her naval background coming out," interrupted Willoughby.

"– but I don't think so."

"Was she in the navy?" asked Harry, who knew little about Willoughby's wife.

"Yes. She was a battleship."

"Willoughby! Stop being naughty!" commanded Rikki.

"Anyone want a drink?" asked Harry.

"No, allow me dear boy, I'm in the chair," said Willoughby.

"No, this one's on me, you can get the next," said Harry. "Same again for you two? Red wine for you Anun?" After nods of assent, Harry went off to the bar.

"Sorry Marmaduke is not coming. He is banging away," said Anun. "He is trying to make up for lost time after going awol this afternoon. I think also you have only got Harry on a short loan as he is due back soon to help to bang some more things, or hold some things or something."

"'Awol?'" queried Willoughby.

"Well disappeared. He said he'd gone for a walk round the village, but he had slipped out without telling anyone."

"Did he avoid the highwayman?" asked Willoughby.

"Hang on, no one ordered a Screwdriver cocktail did they," said Harry sitting back down and looking at the receipt the Steward had given him.

Anun took it from him. "Nor a soup ladle I would imagine, unless they have massively upped the drink sizes here," she said. "This could be interesting to see what drinks the Steward brings. A screwdriver is a type of highball isn't it? That sounds appropriate for a golf club. No idea what a soup ladle is."

"It is a ladle for ladling soup, Madam," said the Steward, arriving with the drinks.

"Oh, we didn't order one of those," said Anun.

"No, Madam. I regret that the receipts have taken a cavalier attitude to the facts. It is the new card system."

"This silly new card system," said Willoughby firmly.

"So I have heard it described more than once, Sir," agreed the Steward. "What is input into the machine is not always the same as what is output from it."

"Can you not fix it?"

"I regret that I am not privileged enough to be allowed to program this new system. That has to be done by the Head of the House Committee."

"Rambo."

"Mr Cyril Ramsbotham. But I believe, Sir, that some members do indeed refer to him as Rambo, although the similarity is not readily apparent to me."

"Have you alerted him? If you can't find him, have a decko in the camel," advised Willoughby.

"I have indeed conveyed that information to him, Sir. I informed him that about a quarter of the receipted items are terminally inexact."

"I don't suppose that half-wit was able to do anything," said Willoughby.

"If you are referring to Mr Ramsbotham as 'that half-wit', he was, Sir. He has reprogrammed the device."

"To no effect, judging by these whimsical receipts."

"On the contrary, Sir, he has ensured that no longer do a quarter of the receipts appear as works of fiction."

"But this one is for soup ladles and screwdrivers which we did not order," pointed out Anun.

"She's got you bang to rights there Steward," pointed out Willoughby.

"As I was saying, Sir and Madam, following Mr Ramsbotham's reprogramming of the device no longer do a quarter of the receipts appear wrong. Now it is half of them. Would any of you members like some cheese-and-onion crisps to go with your drinks?"

"How on earth did Dumbo get elected in charge here?" asked Anun after the Steward had left.

"It used to be oh whatshisname," replied Willoughby, "that friend of Benton's, who was House Chairman, but after his arrest and imprisonment we had to find someone else and Rambo was the only person who stood. The Heads of Committee chairmanship is done on rotation and it is the House Committee's chairman's turn at the mo, so that is why he is chairman of that."

"If I stood for the House Committee could I get elected?" asked Harry.

"There seems to be a lot of work involved," warned Rikki.

"I am not sure," said Willoughby in response to Rikki, "I think Rambo does spuddle. But why would you want to serve on a committee chaired by Rambo?" he asked Harry.

"Oh, I was thinking of being elected chairman of it. I suppose that was a bit arrogantly ambitious wasn't it. I'd have to earn my spurs first in doing some more basic work for the club."

"Well," said Anun. "Didn't you say you changed a light bulb in the office for Mags Murtle when she didn't fancy balancing on a chair."

"I'm not sure that would make the basis of a good election campaign," replied Harry, "Vote Harry: he once changed a lightbulb."

"Cor, call yourself a wordsmith," scoffed Willoughby. "Did you complete it successfully?"

"Yes. It was only screwing in a lightbulb."

"So what you say," said Willoughby, "is that you single-handedly managed the successful upgrade and deployment of a new environmental illumination system to an important area of the clubhouse with no cost overruns or safety incidents."

"I organised the college ball one year. I could talk that up, I suppose."

"And you invented the King Tangents format," pointed out Willoughby. "Which reminds me again that I must see whatshisname about the honours board for it."

"Did Rambo have a background in catering or events management or something?" asked Harry.

"No," said Willoughby. "He worked for a firm of tax advisers. But he got made redundant."

"Oh, why?"

"The firm got a big tax bill it couldn't pay."

"There isn't a lot of maths involved is there, figures and so on, in the House Committee?" asked Harry. "I'm not good at that. Bane of my life at school, the Monday maths test. I couldn't tell you the number of times I failed that."

"That probably explains why you kept failing it," suggested Anun. "Oh, Willoughby," she said, "I never finished what I was saying to you about your good lady, er your wife. I had a chat with her about your diet."

"Did she tell you I no longer need to take a house key with me? I can now get back in through the letter box."

"What does your diet involve?" asked Rikki.

"It involves, shall we say, living off the land," said Anun laughing.

"Living off the land?" queried Rikki.

"Yes, if one of our sheep goes missing we know where to look," said Anun teasingly.

"Pah! As if you'd know how many sheep your mother has, Anun!" scoffed Willoughby.

"I have tried counting them. But each time I do so, I fall asleep," she replied.

"Your mother's sheep are safe," said Willoughby, "for if a man steals an ox or a sheep, and kills it or sells it, he shall repay five oxen for an ox, and four sheep for a sheep. So I'd be in trouble with that equation. Oh, unless I get Harry here to do the sums, then I may be okay."

"At this juncture, I better love you and leave you to go and help poor slaving-away Marmaduke," said Rikki to the assembled company.

"I'll go with you," said Harry.

"In case I encounter the highwayman?" laughed Rikki.

"That's a jolly good idea," said Willoughby. "We don't want to risk that."

"You don't actually believe in this highwayman story do you?" asked Harry.

"Best not to risk it. If Rikki meets the highwayman she would give him such a telling off I wouldn't want to be in his shoes. Or boots. I imagine highwaymen wear boots."

"I don't tell people off!" said Rikki. "Stop telling fibs."

"You're doing it again – telling people off. Two-one."

Rikki stuck her tongue out at Willoughby as she and Harry left.

"I have some good news about your diet," said Anun to Willoughby.

"There can be no good news about my diet, only gradations of bad news."

"I have persuaded your good lady to institute another diet."

"Another! One is bad enough. And to think I used to like you, Anun. Not a lot, obviously, but a bit."

She laughed: "No, it replaces your existing diet."

"So you are saving those poor unborn sesame trees?"

"Something like that."

"The authors of the Boy's Bumper Book of British Trees will be pleased. Or perhaps not – depends if they remembered to include sesame trees in their book. Oh dash – I forgot to ask Half Pint."

"It's the 5-2 diet."

"What's that?"

"It's where you don't diet on five days of the week, and you do for two."

"Is there a 6-1 diet?"

"On two days of the week your meals can total no more than 600 calories. On the other five you can eat whatever you want. I thought it would be more useful and you would enjoy that one more."

"Well I would enjoy five days of it more. What is a calorie?"

Chapter 11

Willoughby was sitting in the clubhouse in a state of repressed excitement. This excitement was not due to what he was currently engaged upon, which was doing a crossword with Brian. "Malaya – that's the 'country formerly seen from the Himalayas'," said Willoughby, "top right corner."

"No, that's wrong," said Rambo, who was hanging around the clubhouse, and who had overheard.

"No, it's right," said Brian, putting in the answer.

"There are various answers to that question," Rambo continued, oblivious to what Brian had said, "depending of course in which direction you are looking. Does it say in what direction? That would be important. It could be Nepal, China, Pakistan, Bhutan, India or Afghanistan. But not Malaya," he chuckled. "Your geography is a bit off I'm afraid."

"No, it is Malaya, as that forms part of the Himalayas you see," explained Brian, "well um just Himalayas in fact."

"No it doesn't. Malaya is now part of Malaysia and it is thousands of miles away from the Himalayas. You cannot see what used to be Malaya from the Himalayas. It would have to be something nearer. As I said, the answer would have to be Nepal, China, Pakistan, India or Afghanistan or Bhutan."

"No, it's not to do with geography, Rambo," explained Willoughby. "It's to do with the letters from it."

"Letters? Well you could post letters from Malaya to anywhere. Well you can't now, of course as Malaya does not exist. But you could have if it did; well when it did."

"'Name of the girl in Milan, Italy'. That's Anita," said Brian to Willoughby.

"How can you possibly say that!" said Rambo. "There must be lots of girls in Italy. Anyway wouldn't it be more likely to be an Italian name? Isabella, Sophia, something like that."

"No, Sofia was a 'girl making capital in Bulgaria'," said Brian. "We had that a few days ago."

"Or it could be 'girl and I sink into couch'," suggested Willoughby.

"That would be equally good," agreed Brian.

"Why are you here Rambo?" asked Willoughby. "Shouldn't you be in your wife's garden shed writing? Or somewhere else organising something. Isn't it time for your afternoon nap in the camel?"

"Well I have indeed been organising things. I am concerned to prevent a potential crime wave in Tangents and I have been taking steps against it."

"Is there a crime wave going on? Well, other than whatever it is that Bent Snivelgate has been doing presumably, of course. Apart from those foxes eating your lunch, which surely counts as more a splash than a wave, have any crimes been committed?"

"It was not foxes! Foxes do not use a knife and fork! I have organised a lecture. It will be held in the clubhouse. It is part of the outreach programme I have been tasked with doing as the Chairman of the Heads of Committee. It is a service the golf club is doing for the neighbourhood."

"You are giving a lecture?" said Brian. "I am um not sure the neighbourhood would consider that a service."

"No, I am not giving the talk. Well, not this one. But it could be the first in a two-part series, and I will give the second one. Mine will be on how to avoid scams. The first talk is about how to prevent burglaries by a group of retired policemen."

"Is that what retired policemen do? That's not good at all," said Brian.

"Yes, it's good," said Rambo.

"How can it be," said Brian. "Former policeman going round committing burglaries. And if they know it is them doing them, why don't they just arrest and imprison them?"

"Good point," agreed Willoughby. "I think the police should institute a better vetting procedure as to who they let into the force."

"They are giving the talks!" explained Rambo.

"Oh, it's part of their community service punishment is it?" asked Brian. "Having to give these talks?"

"No, they didn't commit burglaries Brian," said Rambo. "They just give the talks."

"Then who did commit the burglaries?" asked Brian.

"What burglaries?" asked Rambo.

"The burglaries they are giving talks about," said Brian.

"Perhaps it was those foxes," suggested Willoughby.

"No, Brian," said Rambo, "they are talking about burglaries in general."

"So not in Tangents."

"No, not yet, but we must be vigilant. I am making sure people will be vigilant. Everyone complacently thinks they will never be the victim of crime, that it will not happen to them. That is why I am putting on this talk. You will come to it won't you Willoughby?"

"Sorry old bean, my wife has forbidden me. I am to stay at home that evening, strict instructions."

"Oh, you doing something with your wife?"

"Oh no, she intends to come. But she says I am to stay at home. Firm orders."

"You'll come won't you Brian?"

"Your wife is going you say Willoughby?"

"Yes, indeed. She seems to be very interested in this lecture for some unfathomable reason."

"No, I don't think I will."

"In answer to your earlier question, Willoughby," said Rambo, "I am here to make sure all the food arrives safely from Paddock's Farm. It is part of the extra responsibility I have taken on as Chairman of the House Committee. As Chairman."

"Shouldn't you be liaising with the Steward about it then?" suggested Willoughby as a way to get rid of Rambo. When Rambo did not take the hint, Willoughby added: "I believe the Steward wanted to talk to you about this silly new card system and the receipts it spews out."

"It is a beta test," said Rambo huffily. "There will be bugs in it, that is why a beta test is needed. And we, I, have been entrusted with doing this important test. To find the bugs for the developers, that is why I was able to get such a good deal on the system – we are not paying a penny for it you know. Not a single penny."

"I should hope not. The whole thing's a total mess. They should be paying us compensation."

"Mess! Thank you, Willoughby," said Brian. "That's 26 across – 'where soldier consumes pickle'."

"Yes, I had already done that one."

"Oh, had you? Oh yes."

"But it only goes to show what they say about great minds thinking alike," said Willoughby.

Rambo went off to speak to the Steward: "Willoughby has informed me that you wish to speak to me about an important matter."

"I would not wish to interrupt you, Sir, if you are helping those gentlemen with their crossword. I am sure they are finding your input invaluable."

"Oh, there's no point. They are beyond help. They haven't a clue what they are doing. They are just guessing or putting in wrong answers. They think you could see the Himalayas from Malaya when it's thousands of miles away and then they guessed a girl's name in Milan."

"A girl's name in Milan?" said the Steward.

"Yes."

"No," said the Steward after a thoughtful pause, "I cannot see that one."

"Of course you can't, there must be thousands of girls in Milan. Well millions. Milan is one of Italy's most populated cities. Rome is the most, as you would expect as it is the capital, the capital of Italy that is, and then there is Naples and then Milan I would say, or perhaps Milan and then Naples. Or maybe it's Turin. But it doesn't matter, it doesn't matter. The point is there must be lots of girls in Milan, with lots of different names."

"Oh, is 'a girl in Milan, Italy,' perhaps Sir?"

"Yes of course in Italy which other Milan is there?"

"There are many Milans in the world, Sir. I am given to believe that there are at least a dozen places in the United States alone which are named Milan. And of course the Milan you refer to in Italy is in fact called Milano. It is only Milan in English, which is why one of that city's two Serie A football teams is called AC Milan as it was founded by the English as the Milan Football and Cricket Club. I understand that in 1939 the nationalist government made the club call itself Associazione Calcio Milano. But after the war the club reverted to using the English name for the city in honour of their English roots, which is why the club is now known as AC Milan. It was quite an interesting story wasn't it? But, if the crossword clue is 'in Milan, Italy', I would suggest the answer is Anita, Sir."

"That is what they said! But there must be hundreds of girls all with different names in Milan."

"Undoubtedly that must be the case Sir. However I think that Anita is the answer that the compiler of the crossword is expecting. Perhaps if you have finished helping those gentlemen understand the answers to the crossword, you may be able to look at reprogramming the new system of printing receipts? Some members have been pointing out that the degree of terminological inexactitude to them renders them on the point of pointlessness."

"I have not got time at the moment. It is not a simple task, and I have important duties to carry out this afternoon as Chairman of the House Committee. I have shortly got to go to Paddock's Farm. In fact, I better be going quite soon as they do not know I am coming."

"Do you wish me to phone them to warn them of your arrival?"

"What do you mean 'warn'?"

"Forgive my terminology, Sir, I meant in the sense of informing them of your arrival as it is both unanticipated and imminent."

"No, need. I might as well go now. Do not worry, Willoughby," Rambo called across the room as he left, "I will make sure you get your afternoon tea."

"What was that about?" asked Brian.

"No idea," replied Willoughby. "Perhaps he is finally going to sort out this silly card business. Oh, something I meant to ask you Brian. Anun has a new boyfriend. Well a new official one anyway. She often seems to have a few unofficial ones on the go. He's a property lawyer. He's er um, oh he's a famous cat."

"She is going out with a cat? People are odd, aren't they? There was that woman who married the Berlin Wall."

"No, not with a cat. With someone with the same name as a well-known cat. Oh what was his name?"

"Garfield, perhaps?"

"Nope, wasn't that."

"Steven?"

"Is there a famous cat called Stephen?" asked Willoughby, interested.

"Cat Stevens."

"No, wasn't Stephen. Someone in cartoons perhaps it was."

"Mickey Mouse?"

"Not sure Mickey is a cat – I think the clue's in the name, Brian."

"Oh, yes. I meant that other Disney fella who was a cat – Pluto was it?"

"Pluto's a dog."

"Donald?"

"As in Donald Duck?"

"Yes, that's right," said Brian.

"No, I don't think Donald Duck was a cat either. Mind you, Tommy Tittlemouse was a cat, so you never can tell – animals can be dashed devious at the font when it comes to christening their offspring. Tommy? No, it wasn't that either."

"I suppose she was widowed when they knocked it down."

"Who?"

"That woman who married the Berlin Wall. Swedish."

"No he's not Swedish. Well I don't think so."

"Who?"

"Anun's new chap."

"No, the woman who married the Berlin Wall was Swedish. Marmaduke?"

"She was called Marmaduke?"

"No. Anun's cat – is he called Marmaduke?"

"Nope, Anun's feller's not Marmalade, er Marmaduke."

"No, that Harry's friend the Duke of Marmalade, um the chap who made him the camel. Camel! Of course – that's the answer to 'animal arrived and then left', said Brian writing in the answer. "Never realised Marmalade was a place, but lots of foods are named after places aren't they – Champagne, Prosecco, Gorgonzola, sardines. I wonder where Marmalade is?"

"Orange County?"

"Calvin?"

"No."

"Jock?"

"Jock?"

"Winston Churchill's cat was named Jock," explained Brian, "after Jock Carlisle who gave it to him for his 88th birthday. Apparently the National Trust makes sure there is always a cat named Jock living at Chartwell ever since."

"No, wasn't Jock as I hadn't known about the Jocks."

"Leo?"

"No."

"Kitty?"

"No."

"Mademoiselle Fifi?"

"Pretty sure I'd have remembered if Anun's boyfriend was called Mademoiselle Fifi. Who is Mademoiselle Fifi by the way?"

"John Moisant's cat. He took it with him on the plane when he made the first flight from London to Paris."

"Oh. No, it wasn't a famous cat like that, it was more one of those bog-standard names."

"Lou?"

"No."

"Fido?"

"No. I am sure it will come to me. It doesn't really matter anyway."

"Why are you telling me this?"

"What?"

"I don't know. Whatever it is that you are telling me."

"Oh yes, I was telling you that Felix – Felix! That's his name!"

"Whose name?"

"Felix's name is Felix."

"Well it would be. What um else would it be?"

"Erm, yes, what was I saying..."

"I um have no idea."

"Yes, that's right Felix is a property lawyer and he gave me an idea."

"An idea as to the name of Anun's cat?"

"No, about the 10-year memberships that the club offers."

"Oh those. The Secretary doesn't like them. He says no-one takes them up so he wants them discontinued. I said we couldn't discontinue them while people still have them."

"Do any members have them? I thought you only sold one?"

"Yes, Bob Thompson has one."

"Oh yes. I remember."

"Why, does um Felix want to buy one? Sign him up. That'd be one in the eye for that perisher Pirbright."

"No. What he was suggesting was that if any new homes are built here, as part of the enticement to buy, a 10-year membership could be included. We'd just need to get onto whoever is selling the houses and arrange it. Do you think you and your membership committee would go for that?"

"For what, sorry?"

"For the 10-year memberships. Would your committee be interested?"

"Oh, no."

"No?"

"No, they already have memberships – all of the committee are members."

"No, what I meant –"

"Oh is that the time?" said Brian.

"Yes we have almost reached the sacred time of 4pm when the Steward will allow us afternoon tea. You'll have a spot of tea with me, won't you Brian, though I appreciate you are not normally an afternoon tea person?"

"Sorry Willoughby I have to dash. I'd told her I'd be back by four. I'm taking my wife to the vet."

"You mean doctor?"

"No, to the vet. She um has an eye infection. Sorry, Willoughby, must dash," and, with that, he dashed, leaving Willoughby alone with the crossword. Willoughby was disturbed from his studious activity, which had not yielded any more answers, by the arrival of Harry.

"Ah Harry, what a happy coincidence. I am looking for a companion for afternoon tea – would you be available for the role? I had hoped to cast Brian, but he has taken his wife to the vet as she is unwell."

"Yes I have just seen him. He said you had invited him for afternoon tea, but he's got to drive his wife as she can't at the moment due to an eye infection. Cat is getting its vaccinations apparently. But I regret that I have got bad news for you."

"Oh dear, can't you join me either? I was hoping you would act as lookout in case Mrs C appeared."

"Well as I have never met your wife, I won't be much good as I don't know what she looks like."

"You don't need to know what she looks like. You will be aware of her presence. Birds will stop singing; men highly successful in their fields will be throwing themselves out of first-floor windows; mice will be looking for traps to hurl themselves onto. You will know if she has arrived. Here, if you can't stay for tea, at least provide a service and have a decko at that," Willoughby said shoving the crossword across towards Harry. "I have got stuck. See if you can unstick me please."

"What does your wife look like as a matter of fact?" asked Harry, picking up the crossword.

"Well, it's quite hard to say," replied Willoughby. "Opinions vary."

"You must know what she looks like," prompted Harry after a period of silence.

"Some things one prefers to forget. And of course if I see my wife that normally means she can see me, and that tends to have an adverse effect on her expression. But, well, she looks a bit like a Sherman tank which, having got out of bed on the wrong side, has then received some bad news which has put it in an especially foul mood; although she has a slightly less benevolent countenance than that. You been playing golf – is that why you're here?"

"No, I have been taking Mrs Winsor's baked goods across to the clubhouse."

"Oh splendid, you have been delivering this afternoon's tea treats have you? That is a service indeed. I have been much looking forward to my afternoon tea. What was on the trays? I hope they were groaning with goodies."

"Well there is something I ought to tell you first."

"No, no, whatever important news you have to impart can wait – let me have the maximum time to savour the culinary delights that await me. You can have no idea how I've been looking forward to this. Only if you have lived with a murderer of unborn sesame trees can you have even a notion of the simple joy and pleasure and excitement the prospect of escaping and eating something that was actually designed to be eaten can give. What was on the trays? Start with the cakes – what were the cakes?"

"Er. I think there was a fruit cake as apparently that is always popular here and the other one was more exotic, er, oh yes – apricot, cardamom and chocolate cake was the other one. I think that's what she said."

"Oh that's a new one, I will look forward to that. I think I'll have the fruit cake first – she makes very fine fruit cake. We've always had good fruit cake here, even before Mrs Winsor's time. No surprise it's popular. Scones?"

"Yes. But I must warn you –"

"Homemade biscuits?"

"Yes, she had done some more of the cherry ones. Yesterday's lot were very popular apparently."

"Rightly so, magnificently marvellous are her cherry biscuits. So that will be scones with tea and jam, then some fruit cake and cherry biscs. Oh, of course and some of that apricot, cardamom and chocolate cake – that's a new one so I shall look forward to tasting that. Might have two slices of that if it's as good as I expect it to be. Four o'clock cannot come soon enough. But until then you can entertain with your conversation: you can either tell me more about the wonderful foodstuffs baked by Mrs Winsor or you can tell me what 7 down is."

"Edinburgh Rock."

"You have brought Edinburgh Rock? Mrs Winsor has been branching out, that is most enterprising, though perhaps there will be limited demand here. Maybe for the halfway hut."

"No, that's 7 down – 'swing by capital for food'."

"Oh yes. Excellent. Sorry, you have been dying to tell me something?"

"No melon, no lemon."

"Was that it? I wasn't wanting melon for afternoon tea. But it does make a nice starter for dinner, especially with a bit of Parma ham. And I have milk in my tea, not lemon. Oh, sorry, I see what you mean 'lack of fruits continues despite revolution'."

"Yes. But I have some bad news for you. Rambo came to help me carry the tray across."

"That sounds more like bad news for you. I am sorry. Why on earth was he doing that? I thought that'd be too menial a job for such a grand person as Chairman Rambo."

"He was concerned about the recent spate of food thefts and wanted to make sure the tea things were not stolen."

"Spate? All that has happened is that some foxes ate his lunch once and now he wants to put the whole village on high alert against highwaymen. Did you get held up by any highwaymen on the way over?"

"No."

"Rambo will no doubt claim the credit for that and put the safe delivery of the cakes all down to him providing you with an armed guard."

"He wasn't armed."

"His tongue is a weapon. He has been known to bore men to death with it. No highwayman would go near you with Rambo there. Perhaps I'll have the apricot, cardamom and chocolate cake first, as that sounds most intriguing, and the fruit cake after it."

"Rambo got surprised by a sheep."

"Why, what did it do?"

"It went baa."

"Why did that surprise him? What was he expecting it to do? Moo, bark, tell him a dirty limerick, recite the complete works of Shakespeare backwards in Spanish?"

"Well I think it was more that he was already tense and on edge and well any noise would have startled him at that moment. And, well you know that cattle grid?"

"Yes, jolly tricky to cross if you are wearing high heels I have been reliably informed. You weren't wearing high heels were you?"

"No."

"Very wise. Was Rambo?"

"No."

"Shame."

"But the noise of the sheep, caused him to start and he lost his balance and seemed to have caught a foot in the cattle grid and he went for a Burton."

"Oh dear, was he badly hurt?"

"No. But Rambo was holding the tray."

"Was the tray badly hurt?"

"Well the tray itself is fine, but its contents – well most of them are now at the bottom of the cattle grid I regret to inform you."

"'Most of them'?"

"Well those that he did not fall on and squidge into the mud and dirt that is."

"So how much survived?"

"None of it."

"None of it?"

"None of it."

"What about your tray?"

"There was only one tray – the one Rambo was carrying."

"What a flipping fustilugs that fatuous fool is. Oh who will rid me of this turbulent tea-denying pest? That watboddled dumpelrump as thick as a Tewkesbury mustard, that cream-faced loon, that mafflard, that stuffed cloak-bag of guts, that rump-fed runion, that cumberworld, that roasted Manningtree ox with pudding in his belly whose brain is as dry as the remainder biscuit after voyage and not worth a gooseberry. I only hope no-one lets the zounderkite out tomorrow morning from the camel. Good job you did not design it with a catch on the inside, Larry. You don't fancy putting a padlock on the outside, too?"

"I did not design it! It has nothing to do with me."

"Well Marmalade then when he designed it. Did nothing survive?"

"No. Sorry. Rambo had insisted on carrying the tray."

"He would, the pompous prat. Have you scoured all over, to see if something has survived? Something might have and you could maybe dust it off a little," said Willoughby hopefully.

"It's all been squished into the mud by Rambo landing on it, or fallen down into the cattle grid."

"Could it be fished out of the cattle grid, using a fishing rod or something?"

"No, I don't think so."

"Have you tried?"

"If you're asking: have I tried sitting beside the cattle grid with a fishing line hoping I get a bite from a rock cake –"

"A rock cake? You didn't say that there were rock cakes as well."

"– caked in dirt and mud and goodness knows what – no I have not. But you are welcome to try."

"Do you have a fishing rod?"

"No."

"Mr Keane?"

"Yes," replied Harry and Willoughby simultaneously, both looking up. It was the Steward, who had spoken and who continued: "I regret to inform you that today's baked goods have not been delivered, which unavoidably affects the service we are able to offer members today. I regret it is due to matters that are beyond my control."

"Yes, Barry, er Larry has been telling me. He says Rambo threw the cakes at a sheep because it wouldn't recite Shakespeare to him or something."

"Really? What an excitable and interesting gentleman Mr Ramsbotham is in his habits. I can of course still offer you two gentlemen tea if you would still like it."

For the past minute or so Willoughby had the countenance of a broken man, but at this he visibly perked up: "Can you?" he asked.

"Yes, would that be a pot of tea for two?"

"Oh, I thought you meant the meal afternoon tea," said Willoughby, descending into despondency again.

"Well if you want something to eat with it?"

"I do," said Willoughby eagerly.

"Not for me, thanks," said Harry. "I have got to go back to help Marmaduke. Oh that reminds me, he wants me to ask if you are free for a game of golf tomorrow morning. He's really into the golf course, he has been taking walks around it assessing it and all sorts."

"Yes, do tell Marmalade er Marmaduke that I will be happy to," replied Willoughby, then addressing the Steward: "You were saying you can offer me some food with a pot of tea."

"Yes, I can offer you some crisps if you would like. We have cheese-and-onion ones on special offer."

"No, thank you," said Willoughby firmly.

"I understand from Mr Ramsbotham, Sir, that the halfway hut has been furnished with some snack food."

"I thought it was closed as Mrs English has gone down with the snuffles."

"No, it is just unmanned. There is an honesty box – but only after, I understand, that Mr Ramsbotham had checked that Mr Snivelgate was not playing today."

"Righty ho. Thank you, Steward."

"My pleasure Sir."

After Willoughby had set off for the halfway hut an idea struck Harry: "If there are tea things there, should I go and get some items to bring back here? No-one will be likely to use the halfway hut this time of day. It'll be dark soon."

"No need, Sir, all Mr Ramsbotham has put there is a couple of boxes of cheese-and-onion crisps. We already have boxes and boxes of those here."

"But Willoughby doesn't like crisps."

"Does he not? Oh, shame."

As Harry left the room he passed Abitha Tatsby and Ursula Gibbs coming in. "Good afternoon," the Steward greeted the pair of old ladies. "Can I be of service?"

"We have come for afternoon tea," said Abitha Tatsby,

"I regret to say there has been a problem with today's delivery of cakes and home-cooked biscuits."

"Oh dear, what happened?"

"Mr Ramsbotham was bringing them over from Paddock's Farm, and I have been told, although I have had no way of verifying this information, he got annoyed that the sheep were not reciting Shakespeare, so threw the tray of today's baked goods at them."

"Oh dear, he gets pottier doesn't he? Does he still throw milk jugs?" asked Abitha.

"I have been told, Madam, that when the urge to throw a milk jug comes upon him he takes himself off to the camel in the car park to have a lie down in a dark room until the urge to throw something has passed."

"I was wondering why that was here. Oh dear, it doesn't seem to be working if he is throwing things at sheep."

"Well perhaps it has been working up to a point, Madam. He hasn't thrown a milk jug for some while now, and if he has moved on to tea trays, well at least they are not china and so are harder to break."

"So we cannot have afternoon tea today?" asked Ursula Gibbs.

"Yes, you can, but we have a reduced menu – well it is in essence anything we have left over from yesterday. Is there anything you'd particularly like?"

"Well we had been hoping for a pot of tea for two, scones with cream and jam, two slices of fruit cake, oh and did you say you would like a cherry biscuit dear?" she said addressing this last part to her friend.

"Yes please," said Ursula Gibbs.

"Would any of that be available by any chance?" Abitha asked the Steward.

"Yes, Madam, we happen to have all of these items. I shall bring them across to you shortly."

Chapter 12

"I was told I'd find you here," said Rikki walking up to where Willoughby was lunching on his own in the clubhouse.

"Then your sources were impeccable."

"They were Marmaduke."

"I thought one is not supposed to reveal one's sources?"

"Isn't that just if you're a journalist? Or is it a spy?"

"Then I deduce that you are neither. Or that, if you are, you are a rotten one."

"Excellent deduction, Cornwallis."

"Elementary, my dear Winsor. I take it you have eaten? Otherwise please do join me."

"Yes I have, thank you. How was your golf game with Marmaduke?"

"Most illuminating and entertaining. He has a most unusual technique. I can only surmise that he has misunderstood the rules and believes the point of the game is to lightly brush the golf ball with his club's shadow. Or maybe he is simply a tender-hearted fellow who worries about the pain he may inflict upon the ball, so tries to take it suddenly unawares. Though, in truth, some of his swipes make so little contact that I do wonder sometimes if the ball is even aware that it has been hit. Then at other times he makes perfect contact and sends the ball soaring away in glorious fashion. You never know what you're going to get with him. A most spectacular golfer and one who it is an invigorating privilege to watch in action. We also had a really good chat as we went round."

"Glad you like Marmaduke. I confess I wasn't sure of him."

"How so?"

"He just seems at times a bit, well, shifty I suppose you might call it, or maybe just evasive and, well, sometimes he disappears to quite where no-one knows and without telling anyone. All just a bit odd at times."

"Oh dear, has he not been putting in a solid 9 to 5 shift?"

"No, he has worked like a trooper. He has been really useful, and had lots of good ideas and suggestions. He's been absolutely super at that. We've been very lucky and it's jolly kind of him, as he's doing it all for free and it's supposed to be his break from work so it's a real busman's holiday. I do feel guilty."

"That you don't trust him?"

"No, that he hasn't had a better break from work."

"He's had a couple of rounds of golf, and he has enjoyed going for walks about the village and the golf course at other times. I shouldn't feel too sorry for him. Plus of course he has met me, which I imagine has been the highlight of his stay."

"I think it has been Mumsie's cooking actually. But he said you'd been really helpful. I presume that has been in helping him to improve at golf; he did say he is not very good."

"I am not sure I am the person to ask for how to get better at golf. But I have at least been helpful in spotting where his ball goes. You don't realise quite how many bushes there are on that course until you play with Marmaduke. He has caused me to see the course with new eyes."

"Anun has always said there were several good, big bushes there."

"Shall I bring your puddings now, Sir?" asked the Steward, clearing away Willoughby's plate.

"Please. That was most enjoyable – give my compliments to the chef. It was even better than those delectable chops."

"I will do so Sir. Chef will be pleased. Chef has been perturbed that fewer people have come in to dine recently and has taken it personally."

"Please tell Chef it's not a reflection on the continuing excellence of the food, it's all to do with that idiot Rambo."

"I have, Sir, although of course not in those exact words you understand. It would not be seemly for someone in my position to use such language about a member."

"No?"

"No, Sir. I always call him Mr Ramsbotham."

"I have just come to say goodbye," said Rikki as the Steward moved off in stately fashion carrying Willoughby's empty plate with him.

"Fear not – I am not going. I know Mrs C is trying to starve me to death, and looking at my emaciated form you may believe she is succeeding massively, but I am determined to disappoint her. I am confident that I will – I seem to have form for that. Rest assured Half Pint, I intend to live for ever – or die in the attempt."

"No, soppy, I am the one going. Back to university. I have got to present a paper. On Hogarth."

"Him of Beer Street and Gin Lane, or is it the other way round?"

"No, you got it right. My paper is on 'the effectiveness of Hogarth's use of satire to influence 18th-century society and does his work still have relevance to life today?'"

"He also did that series on an ill-considered marriage, didn't he?"

"Marriage A La Mode."

"I'd say the answer was yes."

"I think my professor is hoping for more than a one-word answer."

"How about: 'yes, most certainly it does'."

"That's still quite short."

"Brevity is the soul of wit so your prof should be impressed how you are immersing yourself in the subject."

"Here are your puddings," said the Steward, placing them on the table in courtly fashion.

"I didn't order a pudding," pointed out Rikki.

"No, Madam, Mr Cornwallis ordered both of them," replied the Steward.

"It's all part of a balanced diet," Willoughby explained to Rikki as the Steward moved off.

"How does having two puddings the same form part of balanced diet?"

"They are not the same."

"Yes they are. You know my method. It is founded upon the observation of trifles."

"Very good, Half Pint. However you see, but you do not observe. They are different types of trifle. One is strawberry; the other, rhubarb and ginger."

"Oh so, they are," said Rikki examining them. "That rhubarb one looks rather intriguing. Still doesn't make it a balanced diet."

"Yes it does, I had two main courses so I need two puddings to balance it."

"I thought you are on a diet."

"I am. I have been put on this 5-2 diet, whereby you have to eat as much as you can on five days of the week as you are not allowed to eat on the other two."

"Are you sure that is how that diet works?"

"Totally."

"Hey, I thought you weren't able to order food on your card. Hasn't Mrs C forbidden it?"

"She has."

"But you appear to have had a mountain of food."

"A wormcast at best. I did not order it: Larry Keane did."

"I hope you have paid him back. He can't afford to buy your lunches. Especially ones the size of yours. He isn't earning much from his writing and he gets nothing for his work on the farm."

"Honestly Half Pint, the way you get names muddled. You are thinking about Harry King, he who has tended loving care to Rik-Pig when you have been away scoffing hot chocolate and buns in St Andrews, by keeping said animal abreast of all the latest football news and deluged in crisps. I am talking of Larry Keane."

"Who's Larry Keane?"

"You could say we came into the world almost like brother and brother, and we go hand in hand, not one before another through the dining room, as a band of brothers, for he that today shares his food with me shall be my brother."

"You don't have a brother."

"I have always considered that to be my brother's loss."

"Hey, this rhubarb and ginger one is rather good," said Rikki, who had picked up a spare spoon and had been sampling it. "Is the strawberry one just as good?"

"I wouldn't know," said Willoughby pointedly, "I have yet to have any of the rhubarb one."

"You'll love it when you do, it really is jolly good. How's the strawberry one?"

"Infinitely better than sesame seeds."

"Oh you're hopeless. Let me check," said Rikki, helping herself to a scoop from the strawberry trifle that was in front of Willoughby. "Yes, it's even better I think than the strawberry one, but let me just double check," and she helped herself to another scoop from the bowl in front of Willoughby.

"Yes," she said, taking another couple of mouthfuls of the rhubarb and ginger one just to check. "You'll love this, it's jolly good."

"Ah Steward," said Willoughby hailing the passing club servant. "I am reliably informed that the rhubarb and ginger trifle is excellent."

"It has proved exceedingly popular with the diners, Sir."

"Yes, it's first class," said Rikki enthusiastically. "Please tell Chef that. Great addition to the menu."

"I will, Madam. But I understand it was something of a one-off. Chef has been concerned about the declining numbers of diners, so has been introducing some one-off items in the hope of enticing people back."

"So please may I order one," said Willoughby.

"You have already had one, Sir."

"No. Half Pint has had one."

"No, we're sharing," said Rikki, "you have the... oh, crumbs, sorry!"

"What do you mean crumbs?" said Willoughby. "There's never any crumbs left when guzzleguts you gets to work; there's hardly any pattern left on the plate either."

"I am sorry Sir, there is no more of that particular pudding left. It has proved very popular, as I said."

"I'm not surprised, it was jolly good," said Rikki. "You'd have loved it, Willoughby."

Willoughby opened his mouth to say something, but at that moment the Secretary swept in: "Ah Willoughby, you've got lunch I see. Your card been sorted, has it? Excellent. I am so pleased," the latter said when he was scanning the room, "Oh dear, I am too late obviously."

"Yes, if you want to eat my lunch: Rikki has beaten you to it."

"Did you have the rhubarb and ginger trifle?" asked the Secretary of Willoughby. "I did. It is excellent. We asked for some to be sent through to the office. No, I am looking for a new member. I was hoping to see him here. But I am disappointed to see there is only you left. Never mind, not your fault. But you may be able to help me," said the Secretary to Willoughby and Rikki. "If you have been dining here, you may have seen him."

"What does he look like?" asked Willoughby.

"I don't know," said the Secretary.

"What was he wearing?" asked Willoughby.

"I don't know."

"This could prove a problem. We have no data yet and it is a capital mistake to theorise before one has data. Insensibly one begins to twist facts to suit theories, instead of theories to suit facts," explained Willoughby.

"You may have met him?" asked the Secretary hopefully. "His name is Larry Keane."

Willoughby dived in to answer, sensing that Rikki was about to say something: "I can honestly say that I have never actually met him."

"Why do you want to see him?" asked Rikki. "What mischief has he been caught up in?"

"What makes you say that Miss Winsor?" asked the Secretary.

"Call it a woman's intuition," she replied.

"I just wanted to check that he really wanted to be a social member of our club," the Secretary said.

"Why are you trying to put people off being members?" asked Willoughby. "I thought you were always banging on about the need for more members, and here we are having caught one and you want to throw him back? Or is there a good reason for this – is he a friend of Benton's? In which case throw him as hard as you can and make sure he lands with a huge bump. Preferably on his head."

"No, I want to ask him if he wanted to be a golf member instead," explained the Secretary.

"Yes, tell him that is a much better thing to be," said Willoughby, "rather than one of the riff-raff that come in here as social members stealing food from the needy."

"Normally we enrol members in the office," explained the Secretary, "but this one was done by Brian and he didn't do the paperwork properly. Well, hardly at all in fact. I had spoken to this chap a few months back as he wanted to become a golf member and I had arranged for him to come and see me on Captain's Day. But he never showed up. Now that he has, Brian has enrolled him as a social member. The chap had distinctly told me he was wanting to become a golf member."

"Then can't Brian tell you what he looks like?" said Rikki, who then mouthed "one-all" to Willoughby.

"Oh you know how Brian is. I saw him yesterday about it, but he couldn't even remember enrolling Mr Keane. He was terribly vague about it all, and then said he had to rush off somewhere because of his wife."

"Yes, he was taking her to the doctors," said Willoughby.

"Oh dear, is something wrong with her?"

"Suspected case of distemper, I believe."

"I am sure Mr Pirbright that with the help of Watson here," said Rikki, "I can crack the case of the absent early diner."

"Hang on, I was always Holmes," complained Willoughby.

"That means it must be my turn now," pointed out Rikki.

"No, the old ways are the best, just as Martin Cowmeadow always tells us. So I shall be Holmes," said Willoughby. "Tell us your story fully, Mr Secretary. Omit no detail that may be of importance. Why do you believe this chap Keane was in here?"

"Because it has come up on his food and drink card that he has had lunch here today."

"Now we are getting somewhere," said Willoughby approvingly. "What did he have to eat? Rikki may have liked the look of it and eaten it for him, and so we might catch him that way. You never know your luck."

"Oh that's just bizarre," complained the Secretary.

"It is," agreed Willoughby. "But she does that, I assure you."

"No, what the system said he had for lunch is just bizarre."

"As a rule, the more bizarre a thing is the less mysterious it proves to be," said Rikki.

"Well, if you must know, it says he had a saucepan."

"That's good, sounds like someone with a hearty appetite – we are piecing together a profile. A saucepan of what?" asked Rikki.

"Just a saucepan."

"Perhaps he is someone with an iron deficiency," suggested Willoughby, "and he was looking to rectify it? So you should be looking for a chap with pale skin, and brittle hair and nails. And probably also chronic indigestion by now."

"Why do you keep saying 'chap', my dear Watson?" asked Rikki.

"Well, Watson," replied Willoughby, "he is called Larry and you know what that is short for."

"Harold, if some people are to be believed, but also Larissa. So this Larry could be a lady."

"There you are, Mr Secretary, Watson here has narrowed down your suspect to either a man or a woman. You see now why I always had to be Holmes. Did this chap, or indeed chappess, have anything else?"

"According to the system: a candle."

"Sounds like he is one of those fellows who was wanting a light lunch," hazarded Willoughby, "but got a bit confused somewhere along the way. Perhaps he does not have English as his first language, hence the confusion? I think you need to be looking for a pale-skinned foreigner, Mr Secretary."

"Thank you," said the Secretary. "You have been as invaluable in your assistance as usual. Please tell Brian if you see him I'd like a word with him."

"I will, and if you see him, Mr Secretary, please tell him I also want to have a word with him: about."

"About what?"

"About – 'Boxing day activity is concerning'. It was the final clue yesterday. It came to me last night when I was having my bath with Ronald."

"Ronald?" queried Rikki.

"My rubber duck. He wears a top hat and has a monocle," Willoughby added as an afterthought, "which I always think is rather overdressed for a bath, but the fellow cannot be reasoned with."

"I think I better talk to the Steward. Perhaps I'll get more sense from him," said the Secretary. "Oh yes, and Miss Winsor, if you see Harry King please tell him to remove that camel. It has been stuck in the car park for days now. I don't know what he was thinking in having it delivered here."

"He didn't," said Rikki.

"He didn't think, did he," said the Secretary, stalking off.

"I deduce," said Rikki, "that this Larry Keane is a fat man who is on a diet. Sounds a bit like you, Willoughby."

"I thought you said a 'fat man', not a perfectly proportioned fellow like me. Or, rather, like I used to be. I am so skinny now that when I put on clothes I look like a washing line. Indeed when I was waiting for a bus recently a lady came out and pinned her washing out on me. Fortunately it was an open-top bus, so her clothes dried in the breeze. Unfortunately I do not know her name to return the garments to her."

"Oh you do fib so," said Rikki. "And you're going to be in trouble if the Secretary finds out who Larry Keane is. It will serve you right for being naughty."

"Oh the Steward won't rat me out. He enjoys annoying the Secretary too much to do that, and our Secretary is hardly one of life's great detectives – he'd even struggle to find out today was Monday."

"Today's Tuesday, Watson."

"Therefore I was perfectly correct in saying that he'd struggle to find out today was Monday. Oh dear, that means tomorrow is Wednesday."

"Excellent deduction my dear Watson, but why is that an 'oh dear'?"

"That is one of my two days. Oh dear."

Chapter 13

Rambo was busy fussing around self-importantly, greeting people as they came into the room at the clubhouse to listen to the talk he had organised on burglary prevention. Not that he had that many people to greet as few people were turning up. But if this had dented Rambo's sense of self-importance it did not show as he stood beside the three men who were there to give the talk.

Rambo had been surprised, but gratified, that three former policemen had come to give the talk. He had presumed it would only be one who would have been sent; but three, he reasoned, was even better. "Well only one of us does the actual talking," one of three had explained to him, "two of us are supporting acts as it were and help out with admin and so on."

"Good evening, good evening," said Rambo greeting the next person through the door, "ah, Miss Murtle how excellent to see you. Come for our talk have you?"

"Yes, well I wasn't going to bother, but then I thought 'why not?' Gets me out of the house of an evening, and there is nothing much on television this evening anyway."

"Delighted to have you along," said one of the ex-policemen, "I hope that you will find it an instructive and useful evening. Please could I ask you to put your name and address on that sheet?"

"Why?" asked Miss Murtle.

"Normally we hand out a booklet at our evenings which has lots of useful info, some handy numbers and so on in it. It acts in part as a recap of the evening, as we know it can be hard to take everything in at one go; however it also includes some extra information and tips we are not able to include in our talk. But I regret we have had some problems with the printers so we haven't been able to bring any with us tonight so we are going to post them out to attendees when we get the next batch in again. Sorry about that. So if you will just put your full postal address down there," he said, indicating the sheet attached to a clipboard.

"Close your mouth," snapped a voice.

"I hear Mrs Wilkinson is here, oh and Mr Wilkinson too of course," said Miss Murtle, a comment vaguely directed towards the ex-policemen, but really to no-one in particular. "And I guess at least one of the Winsor girls must have just arrived." She turned around and she found that was indeed true – Anun had just come in with Harry.

"Please may I ask for your name and address?" said one of the ex-policemen approaching Anun.

"That is very forward of you," she replied, looking him up and down. "Sorry, I am not that type of girl. Hallo Mags, you come for the evening's entertainment?" said Anun turning to speak to Miss Murtle.

"Well there was nothing much on telly," Miss Murtle replied. "But what are you doing here; surely you have got better things to do?"

"Harry was keen on coming," said Anun, "I think he is hoping there is scope for an article out of it, and he asked me to come along to point out Mrs Cornwallis to him."

"Oh is Willoughby coming too?" said Miss Murtle happily.

"No, he has been told he has to stay at home."

"Oh, so we are just getting Mrs Cornwallis?"

"Yes."

"Oh dear."

"Do come and sit with us," invited Anun, "unless you have others who are coming?"

"Thank you my dear. No, it's just me."

"Let's park ourselves over there, that way we can scan the whole audience," suggested Anun. They took their seats while Harry continued to talk to one of the three lecturers by the table.

"Gentlemen, ladies, if we can begin to start, or start to begin, whichever way you want it," said Rambo loudly to the assembled people, laughing at his little word play. He was the only one who did.

Harry scurried over to where Anun and Miss Murtle were sitting and sat down next to Anun. "Has she arrived yet?" he asked.

"Nope. I have been looking out for her and had thought maybe the lady all bundled up and in a head scarf who I glimpsed briefly with a chap I don't know might have been her, but I can't see where they have gone – and I'm not sure that was even her anyway," whispered Anun, as Rambo made his opening remarks.

"...this talk is one of the many things I am organising for the village in my role as Chairman of the Heads of Committee at the golf club," Rambo was saying. "This is the most important committee of the golf club and I am its Chairman. Its Chairman. This talk will be followed by another one. I have not determined the date of it, so do keep an eye out for when the date of that will be announced. I am not sure yet of the date, the date I mean that the date will be announced rather than the date itself, but of course on the date this is announced will be when the announcement of the date that the talk is to happen so they are one and the same thing in one way, although of course they are not the same thing in that they won't be the same date."

"But another thing," he continued, "and you may not be aware of this, but there used to be a local festival in the village called a Taste of Tangents. Not many people know of this, but I do as I am the local historian and have written a book about the history of our golf club which I am intending to have published in the near future. It's just a question of getting the right publisher for such a work. There are some quite interesting stories in it, for instance..."

Much later, and several stories and digressions later, Rambo sat down. He then promptly got up again. "Oh yes, I forgot to mention, for those thinking of entering the speciality section of the Taste of Tangents, which I remind you is to make things using cheese-and-onion crisps as one of the ingredients, the rules of the competition say you have to get your crisps from the golf club. So please do have a thought on that, and please do enter. We will be serving some of these crisps after the talk so please do stay and chat and have some refreshments. Sorry," he said looking across at one of the three policemen, who had stood up and had been expecting to start his talk.

"I hope we still have some time left for our talk on crime prevention," joked the former policemen, to some laughter, "after that introduction by our chairman. But just to introduce myself, as our chairman did not, I am retired policeman PC Kitson, and these are my former colleagues former PCs Emerick and Capstick. Between us we have, well, many decades of service in the police and I would like to share with you tonight some tips for burglary prevention. There are several basic, simple things that any householder can do which involve little or no effort, but which can be highly effective. For instance, who here among you has come here tonight leaving no-one at home? Hands up please."

Several hands went up.

"Now keep your hands in the air please if you have left some lights on at home before coming out tonight? Ah excellent," he said, surveying the audience, "that is Mr and Mrs Wilkinson is it not, and sorry, Sir, I am not sure of your name?"

"Revie," replied the gentleman shyly.

"Now normally we would present some gold stars to these wise and sensible people. They are stars worth having too, as they are chocolate ones, but I am afraid we had a break-in at our offices and the box of these was among the things stolen. So may I invite you all instead to give a hearty round of applause to Mr and Mrs Wilkinson and Mr Revie here."

Harry had taken the chance of the hands going up to look round the room. During the applause he was able to nudge Anun and whisper "is she here yet?"

"She's not in the audience that's for sure. I thought I saw that lady at the back just now with that chap again, but she appears to have disappeared again," Anun had whispered back.

Harry, disappointed, settled back to listen to the rest of the talk. It was proving to be a disappointing evening all round. He had hoped to get an article out of it, but knew that his credentials as a crime preventionist were none, so he needed quotes from someone who would be recognised as an expert if he was to sell an article on it to a publication. But none of the former policemen were prepared to be interviewed by him after the talk for an article, which had taken Harry aback considering that the point of their organisation was to spread the word about how to prevent crime. But they had explained that they had had a bad experience with an interviewer previously, who had caused them a lot of problems and so, no offence, but they had had to institute a firm rule that they would not do any interviews.

Harry had then changed tack, in his quest for an article, and suggested one about their work in crime prevention instead and explaining how this group was available to give talks to local groups. But this had also met with a negative. They explained that they already had a full programme of talks and did not want to publicise themselves further as they were already struggling to meet current demand for their services.

The speaker clearly knew his stuff, but the talk was rather ponderous. It struck Harry that it was as if the speaker had been told he had to talk for a certain length of time, but had not prepared a talk that was quite that long. Harry was not sure why this would be as, if anything, Rambo's lengthy introduction must have reduced rather than extended the time. The speaker had a habit of stopping and asking if anyone had any questions about what he had just said and then would pause for a longer while than was necessary when it had become clear that no questions would be forthcoming. Whenever he did this, Rambo would leap up and also repeat: "Anyone have any questions?"

The speaker was not a natural orator, and Harry wondered why he had been the one of the trio who had been chosen to do, it seemed, all of the speaking; the other two ex-coppers appeared to have gone off somewhere. Harry could not blame them. He wasn't sure what their role in proceedings was exactly, but if it was purely for the pre-talk admin, then he could hardly blame them for not hanging around. Presumably, they may well have heard this exact same talk many times before. Perhaps they had gone to the bar.

Harry's attention had been drifting when he became aware of a commotion. Two uniformed police officers had entered. They walked up to the speaker, who was looking alarmed, and announced that they were arresting him for aiding and abetting burglary. The speaker tried to make a bolt for it, but one of the policemen grabbed him and the two coppers then manhandled him away.

Rambo now had his answer to why three men had come: the other two had obviously gone off to dress up as policemen for this dramatic finale to the talk. Rambo leapt to his feet delightedly: "Ladies and gentlemen, I think we can all agree that was a most fascinating and illuminating talk topped off by the wonderfully theatrical flourish to end the evening – it's a good job these two did not hand back their uniforms when they left the force!" He looked behind him to where the policemen had bundled the speaker off. "Can I now invite our three guests to come back and receive a well-deserved round of applause."

When the trio did not return, Rambo looked surprised, but said: "They are obviously staying in character, but I suggest we give them all a big hand anyway." He continued to speak, reminding people of the cheese-and-onion crisps available and the talk he was planning to give. But few people were paying attention to him in the excited hubbub.

Chapter 14

"Oh, what a sight you are to behold this fine morning. You are looking, if I may so, even more elegant than usual."

"Oh Willoughby," said Miss Murtle, who had been walking along the lane to the golf clubhouse, "what, in this simple thing? You do say the daftest but kindest things."

"As that designer what's her name – a drink comes into it somewhere, er Mary Pickford, no that's not it, Margarita somebody, no that's not it either; well anyway she said 'simplicity is the keynote of all true elegance'. I hear you had a front row seat to last night's excitement."

"Yes indeed, it was all most exciting. I am glad I had come out, especially as on telly all there was was another of one of those dreary crime dramas. Who would have thought it? Well your wife obviously. How did she know?"

"Well she told me all about it over breakfast this morning." said Willoughby, his voice tailing off.

"What was it?" prompted Miss Murtle.

"Fried eggs, a couple of rashers of bacon, some tomatoes, baked beans –"

"Well you seem to have breakfasted well."

"No, that was her breakfast. Mine was sesame seeds and two-thirds of a grape. It is a Wednesday. I got the remaining third of the grape for my lunch, with – "

"No," cut in Miss Murtle, "I meant was what was it that alerted her suspicions as to the true purpose of his talk?"

"Oh, yes, that was from her work in the prison service. There were some bods in the jug who had done exactly this scam before and when she heard about Rambo's talk she recognised the components and thought that perhaps these cons were up to their old tricks. So she alerted the local constabulary and went along in disguise with a plain clothes policeman to have a decko at those johnnies putting on the event and... there was some toast, two slices of it. Brown bread toast.”

“What has toast got to do with the talk?”

“Oh sorry, yes, she went along, recognised one of the pretend ex-policemen and then it was just a question of the plain clothes feller... oh yes she had a sausage too, looked a very nice one...

“Willoughby! Focus on the story!”

“Er what was I saying? Yes, it was just then a question of waiting to find out who they were going to rob. The policemen caught one of the men breaking into the Wilkinsons’ and the other one of the trio in old Revie’s place merrily helping himself to things. No fried slice though: Mrs C doesn’t approve of them.”

“Mrs Cornwallis has become quite the hero of the hour,” said Miss Murtle, “everyone is talking about it and her. You should have a celebration of her catching these crooks, perhaps take her out for a meal or something.”

“A meal! That’s a corking idea – thank you Magnolia, you have once again gladdened, and brought joy to, the heart of an old man.”

“Oh you say the daftest things.”

“I regret I must be away. You have given me an idea. I think I’d better speak to the vicar.”

“Oh, are you not going into the golf club for the committee meeting?”

“That’s tomorrow.”

“No, it has been brought forward, it’s now happening today instead. Same time.”

“Has it? Oh dash it. That’s awkward. Never mind. Yes, I will be there. But must speak to the padre first. No doubt he will be pottering about his church this time of day.

Well, pip, pip," and with that Willoughby made his leave, his exit line being: "that poet Hyman was right when he said 'in manner, in style, in all the things, the supreme excellence is simplicity'."

The vicar was indeed in his church as Willoughby had foretold. "Ah padre, I've just been speaking to Miss Murtle."

"I have just been talking to your wife," replied the vicar.

"I think I got the better of that deal," said Willoughby. An unwelcome thought only then occurring to him, he whispered, looking round anxiously: "She's not here is she?"

"No this was earlier," replied the vicar. "She has become quite the celebrated local figure. The talk of the village. A splendid piece of detection she seems to have carried out and rescued the villagers from that gang of thieves."

"Yes, she has always been very good at stopping people doing things. Particularly at enjoying themselves."

"Harry is busy working on her being celebrated even more widely. I understand he has been onto many national publications and news agencies trying to sell them a story about it. An enterprising young man."

"Oh you've seen Harry today have you?"

"No, I got this from Anun's young man, Felix, as I had a meeting with him today. He was due to come with Anun, but she had to drop Marmaduke off at the station instead as Harry was busy telephoning round trying to sell his story."

"I heard from Felix that everything is going well?"

"Yes, all was most satisfactory indeed. An impressive young man."

"How did your lunch with the Dean go? I forgot to ask."

"Oh that was some time ago now. Yes, that went well enough, thanks. He liked the idea of the Taste of Tangents. He wanted to know more details about its history, so I have been trying to fossick out some more details, but

I am a bit stumped there. I cannot find anything in the church records and I have been asking some of the oldest members of my congregation – such as Abitha Tatsby and Ursula Gibbs – who I believe themselves had elder relatives living here, but they could not remember hearing anything about it."

"Well it's jolly good that I still remembered something about it as otherwise this part of local history could have been lost for ever," said Willoughby. "It's a shame when parts of our history get lost."

"But odd that no-one at all seems to have a recollection of even hearing about it."

"Better talk to Rambo. He does have some info, he was telling me about it."

"I don't think that will be necessary. I am sure he is too busy with his book, his committees and so on."

"Oh no, he won't mind. He is always happy to talk to someone; well, at someone."

"I think it just best if we get on with it. Can I rely upon you to make all the arrangements? I took it from a conversation with Mr Ramsbotham that is the duty of the Taster, not of the vicar."

"Is it?"

"Yes, in my conversation with him I heard that it was the vicar's role to remain impartial and above it all. That is the tradition. So the vicar is forbidden from taking any part in the organising of the tastings. He is there purely to act as a judge, to turn up and sample the wares and approve the person as suitable for providing wares for the festival day itself. The Taster's role is to do all the organising."

"Oh, I thought that you'd help me organise it, padre."

"Alas, much that I would like to share some of the burden with you, tradition appears to dictate that I cannot, and I think we must respect what few traditions we seem to have unearthed from history for this event."

"Rambo told you this did he?"

"This all came out in a conversation I had with him about it. He is our local historian after all. You can check it all with him. He would be most keen to tell you all about it in great detail I am sure."

"No, that's all right. As you said, he is probably jolly busy on his book and his committee work and things; best not to take him away from that. I was thinking of the various tastings before the event that Wednesdays would be the most suitable day."

"Why that day in particular?"

"Well I was thinking some people might be late entrants, as it were, and that the Wednesday the week before would be late enough for them still to enter yet early enough that it gives them time to get everything created for the Sunday service. And, well, it's simpler if we have a set day of the week for all the tastings don't you think?"

"Well, as I said, I cannot get involved, so whatever you decide as Taster goes."

"Oh, padre, I have had another idea for one of your outreach programmes, or whatever it is the Dean wishes you to do."

"Oh yes, pray tell."

"Well I was thinking the church could put on a lunch to celebrate with choice food and sweet drinks or perhaps a feast of rich food for all peoples, a banquet with the best of meats and the finest of wines, that sort of thing."

"Sounds good, but what is it in aid of?"

"Well a celebration of Mrs C's fine work in apprehending the criminals who had organised this talk."

"But that had nothing to do with the church."

"I know that, but this is where your outreach work comes in. You are reaching out to other parts of the village. You would be celebrating the village being delivered from evil. You could bless Mrs C and all who serve and sail in her, that sort of thing."

"I am not sure the church would be the right vehicle for such a celebration. Would not the golf club be more appropriate, as the event was, as I understand it, put on by the club? I would, of course, be delighted to grace such an occasion; indeed I can come and say grace before the meal. That would show the Secretary I am doing things as the club chaplain – attending a club dinner, saying grace, he can't say that isn't me carrying out duties of the club chaplain. But I regret I must leave you now, I have my pastoral parish duties to carry out. I am off to have afternoon tea with Mrs Carmichael."

"She has invited you to tea?"

"Not as such. But she bakes on a Wednesday and if I pop in around tea time she always offers me something."

"Do you want some company?" asked Willoughby.

"Thank you, but that will not be necessary," said the vicar as he exited the church with Willoughby.

"I was thinking that I could come along and tell Mrs Carmichael all about the Taste of Tangents – if she is a keen baker, she might like to be involved."

"That is an excellent idea, Willoughby. That gives me a reason to drop in on her. Well I'll see you for afternoon tea –"

"Oh good."

" – tomorrow afternoon as usual in the clubhouse. Our usual Thursdays."

"Good grief," said Willoughby. But it was not in response to what the vicar had said, but the arresting sight of Rambo travelling in the back of a police car.

Chapter 15

"Ah Martin," Willoughby greeted the Chairman of the Competitions Committee. "Will you be chairing this meeting of the Heads of Committee then?"

"No, why should I? Isn't that Rambo's task?"

"Well ordinarily, yes, but word on the street is that he has been arrested."

"Crikey. Whatever for? You do mean Rambo, not Benton?"

"Yes, Rambo. Details at this stage are sketchy. Could be for anything. Perhaps that sheep has filed a complaint about Rambo throwing cake at it after it refused to recite Shakespeare to him?"

"He did that, did he?"

"So it has been said."

"He gets pottier, doesn't he."

"Or maybe it's for wasting police time about that tomfoolery of going to them to complain of a highwayman eating his lunch."

"Yes, I'd heard that foxes had had it away with his lunch. Ah well, good to see Rambo keeping up the tradition of the House chairman being arrested," said Martin Cowmeadow cheerfully. "Oh heck, do you really think I'll have to chair this committee? It'd have to be this one about what we do about the course. Wouldn't Jerry – he's Greens now isn't he – be a more appropriate soul?"

"Jerry isn't going to be at the meeting. He can't make it due to business commitments."

"Oh dear. Are you sure?"

"Yes, he has given me his proxy vote for the meeting."

"Is it really my duty? Oh heck. No-one is going to be pleased with the outcome, whatever it is, as there are no good solutions. And you know how the members are, they will blame me. Can't we spring Rambo? Get him out on bail? Send him a cake with a file in it or something."

"What type of cake?" asked Willoughby.

"Does it matter?"

"No, I suppose not. On the subject of catering, what food will you be providing for the meeting?"

"Isn't that Rambo's job as chairman?"

"But if you are chairing it instead it's now your choice."

"Well I'd just inherit Rambo's choice whatever that is." Then the two chorused together: "cheese-and-onion crisps!"

"Are you sure, Willoughby, that it's my turn to chair the meeting if Rambo doesn't turn up?"

"Yes, isn't it the Chairman of Competitions who is next in the rotation to chair the Head of Committee? Therefore he stands in for the current chairman if that bod is absent."

"Are you sure it's Competitions' turn next?"

"Pretty sure, old bean. Sorry."

"Well let's go and check with the Secretary. He'll know for definite, or can look it up somewhere. Oh heck – is there an agenda for this evening? I haven't seen one."

"No there has not been one sent round, all due to all the discussions being top secret. But I'd like to add another item on under any other business, please," Willoughby said as the pair of them walked to the Secretary's office.

"Yes, sure," said Martin abstractedly, opening the door to the office, whereupon he saw Brian inside. "Oh hullo Brian, what brings you here?" asked Martin.

"I'm not sure yet. I made a note in my diary," explained Brian, pointing to a note that said 'Hea. Com. Off'. He explained: "I do that as otherwise I can forget things I am supposed to do."

"Oh, like what?"

"Um, I can't remember."

"So why are you here?" asked Willoughby.

"I'm not sure yet."

"Well it doesn't seem to be working too well," said Martin amiably, "if you cannot remember why you are here."

"Well it will when someone explains to me why I am here," replied Brian defensively.

"You've come down to the club for the committee meeting Brian?" asked Willoughby.

"Committee meeting?" queried Brian.

"Yes, the Heads of Committee meeting."

"Oh, that's right! The note in my diary says: 'Heads of Committee in office' in shorthand."

"I think that 'Off', Brian, may signify 'offer' rather than 'office'," suggested Martin. "There's a Heads of Committee meeting this evening to decide on the question of making an offer for Winnie's Place."

"Why is it being held in the office, not the committee room where there is more room?" asked Brian. "Where's Rambo, isn't he the chairman? Perhaps we could ask him to move it to the committee room. Is he in the committee room?" added Brian having looked round the small office thereby establishing that Rambo was not there.

"No, he is in prison," replied Willoughby.

"Oh no," said Brian, "it's not really a prison his wife shuts him in every day. It's just her garden shed. I'm sure she will let him out for the committee meeting."

"No, an actual prison. Well a police cell anyway."

"Oh, are we going to have to go there for the committee meeting?" asked Brian. "I don't imagine there will be much room in there either." Then another question occurred to him: "Why is he in prison?"

"No-one knows yet," replied Willoughby. "Suggestion is that it could be for wasting police time. Perhaps they asked him his name and half an hour later he was still talking and still hadn't got round to telling them yet?"

"That doesn't seem fair," said Brian. "It's very easy to forget one's name. I am sure we have all done it."

"Have we?" said Martin.

"Yes, I am sure you have. Not your actual name, but you know when they ask you for your full name, with all the forenames and whatever."

"Ah Miss Murtle," Martin said when she appeared from the inner office, "is the Secretary in?"

"No, sorry, he has just popped out. Can I help?"

"Yes indeed. It seems that blithering idiot Rambo has got himself arrested."

"Yes, I'd heard that. Oh dear, we don't seem to have much luck with our House chairmen do we? That's the second one."

"Yes, well if he is not released in time, we were wondering who chairs the meeting. Could you look up the rotation order for the Heads of Committee. Who's next in line as it were. It's House at the moment."

"Oh yes, I can look that up. Now, where will it be stated?"

While she was doing that, Martin turned to Willoughby: "Sorry, you were wanting to add something under any other business?"

"Yes, I was thinking that as part of the club's outreach programme it could pay tribute to Mrs C for saving the village from falling prey to this notorious gang of villains."

"You mean a statue or something," said Brian. "A statue of your wife at the entrance to the club could deter burglars."

"And the birds can drop doodoo over it," thought Miss Murtle cheerfully to herself.

"But what if the burglars came in another way and didn't see it?" pointed out Brian.

"Well I was thinking more along the lines of a celebration dinner. One Wednesday quite soon perhaps."

"That sounds a splendid idea," said Martin.

"Well can you add it in at the end under any other business then please."

"Will do. In fact, no, I won't."

"You won't? Why not?"

"Won't be me chairing – as I spy Rambo coming this way. Well that lets me off the hook. It's okay Miss Murtle, thank you, no need to continue fossicking: Rambo has returned."

"Oh dear, has he broken out?" asked Miss Murtle.

"Perhaps he has bored his guards to sleep by speaking at them and he has been able to make good his escape over their comatose bodies?" suggested Willoughby.

"Should we make a citizens' arrest?" asked Brian dubiously.

"Perhaps better to wait to see what the full story is," counselled Martin.

Chapter 16

Martin went into the committee room, where Rambo was standing alone. Willoughby, who had followed Martin in, along with Brian, greeted Rambo with: "Shouldn't you be in disguise? A false moustache, a wide sombrero, that sort of thing? Or hiding out somewhere? What about in the camel, you like it there? No, hang on, that's probably one of the first places they'd look."

"I am glad to see you here," said Martin, "as I had thought at one stage that I might have to chair the meeting."

"Why?" asked Rambo, "I was always going to chair this meeting as the Chairman of the Heads of Committee. I am the Chairman."

"Well we had heard that you were, um, helping the police with their enquiries," said Martin a little embarrassed.

"Yes, that is indeed exactly what I have been doing. And boy do they need help. That police station is most disorganised: its left hand does not know what the right hand is doing. I don't mean that literally of course as obviously a police station doesn't have hands."

"What do you find at the end of the long arm of the law then?" queried Willoughby.

"It was most odd though," said Rambo, "though of course I was glad to help. I had long suspected that, since I am chairman of the most important committee at the club, that they would want to talk to me about the incident as these burglars had been on club premises earlier. But I was most flattered to hear they wanted even more than this, that they wanted my advice and input. They obviously recognised me as someone who has also been involved in fighting and stopping crime. Well a policeman came and collected me and told me he would like me to come down to the police station to assist them with their investigation."

"But when we got there," Rambo continued, "I was interviewed by another policeman who told me I had the right to remain silent. Struck me as a daft thing to get someone to come along and help with their investigation and then tell them that he could sit there in silence. How would me sitting in silence be helping anyone?"

"More than you'd think, perhaps," said Willoughby. "But I doubt that you sat there in silence."

"No, I didn't," replied Rambo, "as obviously I could not help them if I remained silent. But another odd thing was they seemed to have crossed wires – the chap who had kindly driven me there me was not the person who interviewed me, and the person who was interviewing me seemed to be under the impression that I was a suspect for the burglaries, not someone who had come to help the police with their enquires into them. I realised that from some of the odd questions he was asking. He had obviously been told what I had come to the station in connection with, but not why I was there. Well, he knew why I was there but not why I was there if you know what I mean. He seemed to think I had organised the whole thing. He had got the wrong end of the stick entirely."

"Fortunately another policeman came in who I knew from before as he was the chap who I had spoken to about the highwayman. We had had a long chat in fact. He laughed when he saw me there and could see the mistake the other policemen had made treating me like a suspect. He told the interviewing policeman that I was not the brains behind the burglaries. Indeed the policeman was very complimentary, saying I couldn't be the brains behind, well, he said anything but he obviously meant anything criminal – he had obviously recognised that I was an honest person from our previous encounter."

"So they have let you go without charge?" asked Martin.

"Well I offered to stay and help them more," replied Rambo, "but they told me to go. I said I couldn't stay and help them for too much longer as I had this important committee meeting to chair, but I told them I could give them another 10 minutes' help if they wished. But they were quite insistent that I left."

"Rambo, please may I add something to the agenda?" said Willoughby.

"We have no agenda for this meeting as it's all secret what we are discussing, so I will be guiding the committee through the business of the meeting instead," replied Rambo.

"Well, Mr Chairman, anyway in connection with that," replied Willoughby "can I introduce another item for discussion by this meeting."

"Well you can only do that through the chair, and I am not sure that introducing other items would be appropriate as it is a special meeting."

"It was just to suggest that as part of the club's outreach programme the club should host a dinner in honour of the villager who saved the village from a gang of villains," explained Willoughby.

"Oh yes," said Rambo, "that would be a most appropriate thing to discuss and though I say so myself, though perhaps I ought not, a very kind and thoughtful act. Yes, I am happy to include that. But it would be a bit embarrassing, so would you want me to stand down as chairman and perhaps leave the room?"

"Yes," said the Chairman of Estates, who had just come in and not heard any of the prior conversation, "that would be an excellent idea."

"Why?" asked Willoughby of Rambo.

"Well I was the person responsible for getting these criminals caught by putting on that talk, so obviously the dinner is in honour of me. I was the one who drew the crooks out. Be embarrassing me chairing a meeting about deciding to have dinner in my honour."

The Chairman of Estates harrumphed: "No, you are the fool who drew them here in the first place. You are responsible for the crime wave at Tangents."

"Yes, all because of you, someone broke into my house," complained the newly arrived Wilko.

"You mean Wilko that someone breaking into your house," said Rambo, "was apprehended and arrested all because of me."

"I was meaning my wife, Rambo," said Willoughby. "The dinner would be in honour of her. She was the villager who spotted the scam and alerted the police."

"Oh," said Rambo. "Well in which case I can stay and chair. As I said, that is a thoughtful act but I don't think it would be appropriate to host a dinner, well not the club – perhaps you could take her out to dinner, just you and her."

"Perhaps that group those crime prevention lecturers are part of could host the dinner?" suggested Brian. "They are keen to promote crime prevention and I was told they give people chocolate bars for doing so. So perhaps they would like to give people some dinner, too?"

"No, Brian, they were the people who committed the crimes," pointed out Martin.

"Oh yes, that's right, No, they would not be the right people to put on the dinner," said Brian. "Unless they can get bail, like Rambo has."

"Well if you think the club is not the suitable vehicle for such a dinner, Rambo," said Willoughby, "I am sure the vicar will be delighted as he was talking to me about planning to put on a big celebration dinner for the village for Mrs C. But we thought the golf club would be the better host. But if the golf club doesn't want to do so, then the vicar would be free to do so."

"No, we can't have the church doing it," complained Rambo. "What has it got to do with them? I put on that talk, not the vicar."

"Well I think it comes under the heading of delivering us from evil, that sort of thing. Plus he is the club chaplain," pointed out Willoughby.

"Hallo, what are we all discussing?" asked the Chairman of Fundraising, who had just walked it. "Oh what are you doing here Rambo? I had heard you'd been arrested for sheep worrying or something?"

"We were just discussing a dinner," said Willoughby. "To honour my wife for her work in catching these thieves. It could be a fundraiser for the club, although we would not be marketing it as such."

"Fundraiser?" said the Chairman of Fundraising, leaping at the word.

"Yes, but Rambo is against it," said Willoughby.

"Why on earth, Rambo? The club needs all the funds it can get at this time more than any. I am sure they will let you out on bail for it. Anyway, aren't you already out on bail if you're here?"

"I never said that I was against it," complained Rambo, "and I am not out on bail. I was not arrested. I was helping the police with crime prevention. I think the golf club should put on the dinner and I can give a talk at it about the importance of crime prevention and how to avoid being conned as a further part of my help to the police. Plus if Mrs Cornwallis cannot make it for any reason, I could stand in for her as guest of honour as it was me who is putting on these talks."

"I don't think we should have lectures by you at the dinner," said the Chairman of Fundraising. "We want to sell as many tickets as possible."

"Totally agree," said Willoughby, "anyway Rambo aren't you planning this as separate talk?"

"Well I am, and I have ordered some extra copies of the book in readiness."

"Oh you've finally received it then? Is it indeed as good as they say?" asked Willoughby.

"No, I haven't yet."

"So why have you already ordered more?"

"I want to make sure they arrive in time so that I can give them out at the talk. I thought it rather unprofessional of the lecturers not to have those booklets of theirs to hand out at their talk. I am not going to repeat their mistake. I could still do the other talk but I could include some bits from the talk at the dinner."

"No," Martin said, "I think that will just confuse things. Just make it a celebration dinner. No need for crime prevention lectures. But someone will need to give a brief speech of welcome of course."

"I could do that," said Rambo.

"Is it a lunch or a tea, as it will be teatime by time you have finished," said the Chairman of Estates.

"What about the Duke of Marmalade? suggested Brian. "We could reintroduce the aristocratic involvement that the club hasn't had since Lord Hankley's days. That'd be fun."

"Who on earth is the Duke of Marmalade?" demanded the Chairman of Estates.

"He has been holidaying here, and playing our course," explained Brian.

"I doubt that he'll be available," said Willoughby, "as the padre told me he had left today. The vicar could conduct a prayer beforehand in his role as club chaplain. Then as it's traditionally the Captain's duty to give the welcome speeches at club lunches, I suggest we just stick to tradition."

"Yes," agreed Martin, "the old ways are the best."

"I could give a speech introducing the Captain," suggested Rambo.

"Well as it's a fundraiser, it would be the Chairman of Fundraising who'd do the introduction of the Captain if you really think such an introduction is needed Rambo. Do you really think the Captain needs to be introduced?"

"No, he doesn't," replied Rambo. "Well I think everyone is here. Shall we start? This meeting is to decide what to do about our golf course. Now we have had various proposals put forward, and I understand that there have been various unofficial discussions held and, as a result of these, I sense that there is probably a majority opinion in this committee that we should explore the possibility of buying Winnie's Place and using the land there to build two new holes."

"Hang on, who is going to design these new holes?" asked Wilko.

"We don't need to worry about that at this stage," suggested Willoughby.

"But before we can go down this route," continued Rambo, "this committee will need to sign off on the decision to approach the owner of Winnie's Place, or WP as I think we could call it so as to save time. Or does that sound too much like WC and would that cause confusion? But I think it will save time if we call it WP rather than Winnie's Place each time, so I suggest that is what we do throughout our discussion, unless it gets too confusing. I had thought perhaps we could have used the abbreviation P of W to denote Place of Winnie's, but of course that sounds a bit like POW and that in itself could cause confusion, plus of course the house is not actually called Place of Winnie's but Winnie's Place, so I think we should stick to WP. So this meeting has been called by me as the Head of the Heads of Committee so as to allow everyone to express an opinion as to whether we buy WP, that is WP standing for Winnie's Place, or rather I should say, make an offer to buy WP and to have a vote on the matter. By 'we' I do not mean this committee of course, but the golf club, you understand."

As the meeting continued, Martin was glad he was not chairing it, especially as it was playing out. He was far from convinced such an important decision should be made in this fashion. A meeting to decide whether to buy some new land and build new holes on it was being held without the Chairman of Greens present, and also, he realised, looking around the room, without the Chairman of Finance either. He had also noticed that, next to him, Brian appeared to have fallen asleep. However, as that was probably the most useful contribution Brian could make to this, or any, committee meeting, Martin did not nudge him awake.

"Should we totally discount the option of dropping down to a nine-hole course, and selling off some of the spare land for housing to build up some reserves for the golf club?" asked the Chairman of Fundraising.

"That would knock out the chance of having shotgun competitions," said Willoughby, "as we could only get groups onto nine holes simultaneously, not 18, so shotgun competitions would have to be dropped from our competition schedule."

"Is not being able to have shotgun competitions that big a problem?" queried someone.

"Yes it is," replied Willoughby. "Our shotgun competitions only exist so we all finish together so we can all have a big slap-up meal after. Without shotguns bang goes these dinners. It's already hard enough getting a meal round here with this silly card system."

"Going back to the matter someone raised earlier about the design of these proposed two new holes on the Winnie's Place land," said the Chairman of Fundraising, "would this require extra fundraising or is there money allocated for it? I ask as I had an interesting talk with that young lady who walks her little white dog across a field beside our house. Cute little thing."

"Yes, she is," agreed someone else. "She enjoys a cuddle and will often lay on her back so I can rub her chest."

"Will she b'gad!" said Wilko. "Where does she walk?"

"Yes, well I think she knows I will normally give her a biscuit afterwards."

"Oh," said Wilko, "you mean the dog?"

"Who is offering biscuits?" asked Willoughby, coming out of his reverie about some of the fine shotgun suppers of memory.

"They are dog biscuits, Willoughby," said Brian, who was in fact awake.

"Oh, dog biscuits. Damn," said Willoughby. "Still, did someone say they were offering round dog biscuits?" he asked looking round the room hopefully.

"What has this dog got to do with the design of our new holes?" demanded the Chairman of Estates.

"Are the new holes going to be doglegs?" asked Brian.

"Oh, sorry," said the Chairman of Fundraising, "she was telling me of a competition a magazine had had to design a new hole. It was won by someone who went on to become a famous course designer. Could we try something similar as a cheap way of doing it? Avoid a need for fundraising.”

“What – get the club chaplain to run a competition in the parish magazine?” scoffed the Chairman of Estates.

“No, I was thinking Harry writes for Golf Fortnightly, maybe he could interest them in running a competition?”

“Aren’t we crossing that bridge before we have got to it?” said Willoughby. “We haven’t even got the land yet.”

“But it is worth considering when we do come to it,” suggested the Chairman of Fundraising. “Do you think Harry would help us?”

“Harry is always a very helpful chap,” said Willoughby, “a great addition to the club. We are jolly fortunate to have him as a member.”

“If we are now discussing how to design the new holes on the land, that suggests we have de facto accepted that we want to buy the land,” said Martin, “so shall we put it to a vote Mr Chairman?” suggested Martin.

The committee voted to make an offer for Winnie’s Place.

“Okay, who do we get to approach the owner to buy the land?” asked someone. “Is this a task for the Secretary?”

“I think this is a matter for a senior committee member, not the Secretary,” said Rambo. “The chair of a committee.”

“You mean you, don’t you Rambo,” said the Chairman of Estates. “No offence, but you’d be the last person I’d suggest for such a task.”

“Why?” challenged Rambo.

“It’s only because you are a total idiot – again no offence. Some of my best friends are idiots.”

“They’d have to be,” remarked Rambo.

“I would suggest the Chairman of Finance,” said Martin hurriedly, “as it’s a financial matter.”

"I agree," said Rambo, to the surprise of the group.

"Shame he's not here," said Martin pointedly.

"The Chairman of Finance is not at this committee meeting as I have sent him off to see the owner of WP," explained Rambo, "as a good chairman can sense what the mood of a meeting would be and act decisively. I thought it best that we get on with it and not flaff around. I am not one for flaffing around, or for making things take longer than they ought. Oh no, that has never been my style: I like to say things simply and succinctly and get on with things. That has always been my way. Always has been. Never liked people who are long winded, and so I am always keen, and alert you might also say, to ensure I never do that. The Chairman of Finance is meeting with the owner now, and I expect him to return soon. Shall we adjourn next door while we wait for his return?

After they had done so, Martin went up to Willoughby. "Oh, I've just seen that the honours board for the King Tangents is up. Well done."

"Yes, I got Marmalade, er Marmaduke, to erect it," replied Willoughby. "Everyone seems to think it's some other committee, so I reckoned everyone will just think that someone else must have authorised it."

"Do you know, I think it was our committee that was responsible for it in the first place," said Martin.

"That's the spirit Martin. Stick to that."

"No, I genuinely think it was."

Chapter 17

At the same time that Martin was noticing the board for the King Tangents competition, Harry was rushing across the club car park in a state of agitation. The Secretary saw him out of his office window and came out to see him.

"Ah Harry, I want a word with you. It's too bad, it really is."

"Yes, it's awful isn't it. Absolutely terrible."

"Well I am glad you agree. But what are you going to do about it?"

"What can I do now? It's too late."

"Well you can get it moved! I asked you to move this camel ages ago, but it's still in the car park. I must be firm about this, and tell you that you must get it moved straight away. This car park is for golfers, not a dumping ground for wooden animals."

"Yes, yes. Well I must be away, I've got to see someone urgently," said Harry rushing off.

The Secretary returned to his office. "I think that may finally have done the trick, Miss Murtle. I have told Harry King he really has to get his camel moved. It really is a liberty him leaving it here so long."

Harry meanwhile had met up with Willoughby. "Can I have a word?" he asked. "In private."

"Of course, old boy. Step outside. You brought news from Anun?"

"Anun, no, why?"

"Oh. It was just that I was expecting to hear from her. But unfortunately I have got roped into this pointless committee meeting."

"No, it's about Marmaduke."

"I thought he'd gone home? He doesn't want another

game of golf does he? Is there a bush he hasn't yet explored? He's been in more bushes than Anun."

"It's awful – Marmaduke has been working with Benton. That is why he was keen to come here. He wanted to pitch for building contracts with Benton."

"Yes, I had twigged that on the first day."

"You knew?"

"He seemed remarkably well-informed about the business of the 10th and 11th holes. But what really gave it away was when I mentioned Benton and he replied calling him Benton Snivelgate, when I had not given his surname." Then Willoughby added: "And Half Pint has the cheek to think I should become Watson."

"But this is awful. Absolutely awful."

"He's not still working with him."

"I don't know. I presume so."

"No, that was not a question, but me telling you he is not. Look upon it like the parable of the fatted calf, which the vicar was telling the half dozen of us last week, about how there is more joy in heaven over one sinner who repents than over ninety-nine righteous people who do not need to repent."

"That is not the parable of the fatted calf," said Harry distractedly. "That was when a father put on a feast for his wayward son who had returned. The sinner repenteth bit is about a shepherd who finds a lost sheep and is happier about that than the 99 he hasn't lost."

"Is it? Oh, I was sure food came into it somehow. Perhaps I was thinking of Rambo throwing all those rock cakes at Mrs Winsor's sheep if the vicar had been speaking about sheep – my mind can wander during his sermons. I always felt sorry for the son who had stayed behind and knuckled down all those years and didn't get a feast, as he deserved a feast every bit as much, if not more so. Talking of people undeservedly getting feasts put on in their name, Mrs C is getting one from the club. On a Wednesday soon I hope. Do come along."

"Those times Marmaduke has disappeared after lunch and come back saying he had just gone for a walk around the village, he had been going off to see Benton," lamented Harry.

"Well that's not something you would want to do on an empty stomach," replied Willoughby. "Mind you, what would one want to do on an empty stomach, apart from enter a restaurant perhaps. Then again, some of us are forced to do everything these days on an empty stomach. I pray daily to God to give me my daily bread, but either God's gone a bit deaf – and I suppose he must be getting on a bit by now – or maybe it's just that he is no match for Mrs C. You can't necessarily blame him: she is a formidable opponent."

"I feel such a fool," groaned Harry.

"Not at all: you have been most useful."

"Yes, to blasted Benton. Still at least the club can still buy Winnie's Place as Marmaduke didn't know that the club plans to buy it."

At that moment they were disturbed by the Chairman of Finance coming back to the clubhouse. "Ah, what is the news about Winnie's Place?" was Willoughby's eager greeting to the chairman.

"Not good, I regret: Winnie's Place has already been sold. We were too late."

"Oh hell," said Harry.

"Or even oh double hell, as the Secretary might say," replied the Chairman of Finance.

"To Benton?" asked Willoughby.

"No, it's to a company called Banglenote Invest."

"Is it all definitely signed, sealed and delivered? Or could the sale still fall through?" asked Willoughby.

"No, it's actually been sold. It's an actual completed sale. Lady said the money from the sale has arrived in the account and everything. Seems she had some hotshot lawyer on the case forcing everything through. The deed is done, I regret. Ah well, I better go and tell the meeting the news. Aren't you supposed to be in this meeting, Willoughby?"

"We had adjourned, while awaiting your report from the frontline. I suspect Rambo had been planning a big theatrical reveal, but I think he expected you back earlier."

"Yes the lady offered me some tea and cake so it took longer than expected."

"Cake?"

"Yes, but that is not important, what is important is that our plans to buy Winnie's Place are now in tatters."

"Yes, quite. What sort of cake was it?"

"Ah well, I'd better go and tell the committee," said the Chairman of Finance glumly.

"I didn't tell Marmaduke, promise," said Harry, after the Chairman of Finance had gone in. "It can't have been from me if he found out. I am sure of that. I never told or spoke about it when he was near and could overhear. Oh dear, I am going to be public enemy number one as I introduced him to the club. Oh dear, and you have been playing golf with him, sorry. They may view you as guilty by association."

"Don't worry Harry, everything will be alright and you will emerge as the hero of the hour, just trust me. But be checked for silence when we go in."

"Not even you could wrangle this one, Willoughby."

"Ye of little faith, why are you so afraid? It's time to calm the waters and spread sweetness and light. Lead on Macduff."

"Duffer more like," said Harry miserably.

Chapter 18

As Willoughby walked in, he heard the Chairman of Finance speaking to the assembled people: "...so it is now owned by a company called Banglenote Invest."

"Odd name for a company," said one of those gathered around him, "sure it's not 'Investments'?"

"No, it's an anagram," said Brian. "Oh the crafty devil."

"Can't we just buy the land off Bangle instead?" asked one of the committee.

"Even presuming that they'd be prepared to sell, they'd no doubt want a decent profit," pointed out the Chairman of Finance, "and what they have paid for it significantly exceeds what we were planning to offer, and even that figure – well that would have been a tight squeeze as we couldn't get the favourable lending rate from the bank that we had hoped for."

"Miss Gillgrass never owned the property. She was the tenant," remarked Willoughby, "and after she moved out she continued to manage it for the owner. It was actually owned by her cousin."

"So how could she sell it then, if she didn't own it?" said Rambo. "We have got her! The deal is illegal! The deal is illegal, so we can still buy Winnie's Place. I mean WP."

"How?" pointed out Martin, "we know that this company what's its name, Bangle Investments –"

"Banglenote Invest," Brian corrected him.

"– will pay much more than we can for the property. We still get outbid."

"Could we rent it off the new owners?" suggested Wilko.

"I doubt we'll get a good deal there," said Brian. "As the name of the company is an anagram of Benton Snivelgate, I think that tells us who we'd be renting it off."

"Oh hell. Is it? Are you sure?" asked the Chairman of General Purposes.

"Yes, Benton has bought Winnie's Place," said the newly arrived Anun, looking gleefully at Willoughby as she said so. "It's been confirmed by the lawyer working on the deal."

"Hallo Anun," said Willoughby, "everything okay?"

"All absolutely tickety boo squared with knobs on, as you might say," she replied as she sat down, carefully arranging her voluminous skirt as she did so.

"So we're back to square one," said the Chairman of General Purposes with a resigned air. "We'll have to have a 16-hole course or pay blasted Benton his exorbitant rent."

"Or we could drop down to nine holes and sell some of our land for reserves," said the Chairman of Fundraising, "that would raise some useful funds at least." But there was no enthusiasm from the group for this idea.

"Benton must have found out that we wanted to buy Winnie's Place. I wonder how he did that," mused Martin.

"Need you ask?" snorted the Chairman of Estates. "Rambo – you can never stop that mouth of yours spewing out words so you obviously let the cat out of the bag."

"I haven't," shouted Rambo. "I have never even spoken to the man. Well, not recently anyway. Obviously I have spoken to him, but not recently. Not recently I haven't."

"Lucky devil – I wonder how he achieved that, perhaps he could give us tips?" said someone at the back of the group, a bit louder perhaps than he had intended.

"No it wasn't Rambo who told Benton – that was Marmaduke," interjected Willoughby.

"But how on earth did he know? Who told Marmaduke? Rambo was that you?" demanded the Chairman of Estates.

"No, I did," replied Willoughby. "As I wanted him to tell Benton. You probably don't know, but Marmaduke came here to work in partnership with Benton as he wanted to build any houses Benton had planned or, as it turns out, that anyone has planned in and around Tangents."

"Why did you want Benton to know?" asked Martin.

"Because I wanted Benton to buy Winnie's Place. It was me who is selling Winnie's Place. Or, rather, not me but the estate of Godfrey Flower because Miss Gillgrass may have lived there many years but she was never the owner, as I said. It was owned by Godders and I have become co-executor to Godfrey's will, so it has become our responsibility to sell Winnie's Place. As you can imagine, after that terrible business there, it has been jolly hard to find a buyer, and even were the golf club to pay something for it, that offer wasn't going to be enough. But this way we have got Benton to pay far more than we could ever have dreamed of that we'd get for Winnie's Place."

"So you have been doing this all for your own selfish reasons, Willoughby," Rambo shouted, "and acting as a double agent."

"There's no need to shout," said Martin.

"I am not shouting!" Rambo shouted at him.

"Yes," admitted Willoughby, "a double agent has been at work, but that person is not me."

"So," said Rambo, "while many of us have been working away for the good of the club, you have been feathering your own nest at the expense of the club. Does loyalty mean nothing to you? I hope you will resign from my committee now after your treachery."

"I think you will find, Rambo, that it is the club's committee not yours," said Martin, "and perhaps we ought to let Willoughby finish before leaping to conclusions?"

"What more is there to say?" shot back Rambo, who then made a point of looking deliberately at the Chairman of Estates: "It is Willoughby to blame, not me. Even those idiots at the police station would be able to work that one out without needing to call on my help."

"The money from the sale of Winnie's Place does not go to me, but to his cousin Miss Gillgrass and to the golf club," said Willoughby.

"The golf club?" chorused at least two of those present.

"Yes, the golf club. Godfrey specified in his will where the sums raised from divesting parts of what turns out to be quite an extensive portfolio of property and shares are to go, and part of the proceeds of the sale of Winnie's Place will go to the golf club."

"So we can use it to pay Benton's exorbitant rent for the 10th and 11th holes?" suggested the Chairman of Finance.

"That will be up to a meeting of the Heads of Committee to decide," said Rambo. "As chairman I shall convene a meeting at an earliest convenient date for us to consider and I will circulate briefing papers in advance."

"No, we cannot," said Willoughby addressing the Chairman of Finance's point. "The money is for capital expenditure only, not to fund running expenses. Godders had stated that quite clearly – he wanted to add something to the club, not underpin its running costs. Also, he appointed me as executor of this part of the will, so it is entirely up to me how it is to be spent, not any committee, so Rambo's insatiable desire for cheese-and-onion crisps will have to be funded elsewhere."

"I could not say anything before, as I didn't want any leaks, as I feared a blabbermouth, might let the cat out the bag," Willoughby continued, looking pointedly at Rambo, "but the club could not build two new holes at Winnie's Place. That would have required knocking down the house, which cannot be done as there is a protection order on it.

So even had the club bought the land, we could not have used it to build those golf holes."

"Why didn't you tell us all this in the first place?" complained Rambo.

"Because if it became widely known, then Benton would have been put off buying Winnie's Place and we needed someone to buy it so the club could get the money to build our two new holes. Incidentally, I have spoken to someone who has studied this field and, even had we been able to purchase Winnie's Place and get the protection order overturned, we may well have ended up short of the readies to build the holes as it would have been a more expensive process than you may have thought."

"I had no knowledge that this plan would succeed," continued Willoughby. "I just had to hope Benton would be so keen to get one over the committee that he'd dive in and buy the house before we could and so not have the time to do the full due diligence. It was not obvious that there is a protection order on the place. Indeed, we did not realise it had one at first – it only came to light as Gilly had been planning to knock down the house herself and build something new there as she hankers after doing some property development. But she had to abandon that idea. Fortunately she has found somewhere else better locally where she can build."

"Incidentally, why Benton was probably so keen to cut off our Winnie's Place option," continued Willoughby, "is that – and I have got this from Anun's Felix, who is a property lawyer – he would be unlikely to get planning permission to build houses on the 10th and 11th holes due to lack of suitable access to that plot of land. Benton probably also realises that, so he needs the club to keep renting the land for the 10th and 11th holes off him."

"Are we sure Benton cannot back out of it when he finds out he has been conned?" asked someone.

"He hasn't been conned," replied Willoughby. "He has simply bought a house that has long been up for sale. No-one has conned anyone."

"In answer to your question," said Anun, "no, Benton cannot back out of it even if he wished to."

"How do you know?" challenged Rambo indignantly.

"I have been involved in this deal," replied Anun sweetly.

"Yes, Anun is quite correct. It's all legally watertight," confirmed the Chairman of Finance. "The lady, er Miss Gillgrass, said that Banglenotes are now the owners. The deed is done."

"This is where we need to thank Harry King," said Willoughby, "for his most excellent work on behalf of the club. He is truly the hero of the hour here. It was he who got his cousin involved with Benton, so as to be able to persuade Benton to buy Winnie's Place, and to do so in such a hurry that the protection order would not likely come to his attention."

"But what happens when Benton discovers the protection order?" asked Rambo.

"It's too late. Felix has made quite sure that the contract is watertight on that score and that Benton is lumbered with it," Willoughby said, while Anun nodded beside him in agreement.

"Felix says in time Benton will probably be able to get the order overturned," added Anun, "and so could build on that land. But until that happens he can't do anything with the property and the land, just as the club could not have."

"So I suppose we have to renew our lease for the 10th and 11th holes at Benton's price," grumbled the Chairman of Finance. "Or do we try and call his bluff and demand he lowers his rental fee if we now reckon he can't develop that plot of land? See if he blinks first, as it were?"

"Another option," said Willoughby, "is to rent some land elsewhere. I have been working with a landscaper who has drawn up plans for a couple of new holes which I think would suit us very well – rather good holes they could be, much better than the dreary 10th and 11th ones. I have them in my satchel which is in my car, if you'd be so kind, Harry, as to fetch it," he said handing Harry the car keys.

"We do not have any more land," said Rambo dismissively. "That was why we were having to buy Winnie's Place, I mean WC, er, WP."

"Mrs Winsor says we can rent some of hers, and at the same rent we are currently paying Benton for his holes – plus a bit for inflation, of course. We can build two holes on there. The rent we know we can manage and the cost of building the holes will be paid for by Godfrey's bequest."

"What happens to the halfway hut?" asked Martin. "That is also on the land we are losing."

"At the moment Greens don't have anyone to run it," said Rambo. "It is Greens, not House, the halfway hut. A lot of people don't realise that," he said defensively.

"Yes, if we don't have a halfway hut, where will we store all those blasted crisps Rambo keeps ordering?" chirped the Chairman of Estates.

"As you will be able to see when the plans arrive," said Willoughby, "we have rejigged the order of the holes a bit to incorporate these two new ones, but I hope everyone will agree that this re-routing works and, under it, the first of the new holes would still end up being the 10th, so that would be the perfect place to build a halfway hut. Godfrey's bequest can cover building that, too."

"But Greens don't have anyone to run it," said Rambo.

"I was thinking that the club should try to persuade Mrs Winsor to take it on," replied Willoughby.

"The Greens Committee have already asked her," said Rambo, "and she said no. You again haven't done your research properly Willoughby."

"That was to run the existing halfway hut, where its inaccessibility is a particular problem for Mrs Winsor after her accident. But this new halfway hut obviates that, so perhaps we should ask again?"

"That would be a capital idea," said Martin. "Do you think your mother might be persuaded to reconsider, Anun?

"Yes, if the hut will be on our land. Mummy is going a bit stir crazy not being able to get out and about so much since her accident."

"Yes, currently she only really sees Harry and the pig and the pig is moving out," Willoughby explained to Martin, "so she won't even have the pig to talk to."

"Oh we're getting a new one," said Anun, "Rikki says seeing how devoted Harry has been to the pig, she has got another one for him." Then to the group she said: "I am sure Mummy could be prevailed upon to run this new halfway hut for the club as well, if the terms are right and that is what the club committee want?"

There was general agreement to the idea of asking Mrs Winsor if she would take on the halfway hut. Her baked goods were highly popular in the clubhouse.

"Okay, that's agreed then," said Willoughby, "we'll get Jerry Best, as he's Chairman of Greens now, to see what can be arranged. I am sure he can sort something out."

"Hold on, I am chairing this meeting, not you," said Rambo indignantly.

"Oh is it still the meeting?" said Willoughby. "We seem to be milling around in the bar instead? Anyway, this is a Greens Committee matter, not a House one, and I am standing in as proxy for Jerry at the moment."

"Yes, it's a Greens matter," agreed the Chairman of Estates, "so nothing to do with you Rambo. Go ahead, Willoughby, it's an excellent idea."

"Oh, thanks," Willoughby said to Harry, who had just returned and handed over the satchel. "I have here some rough plans," said Willoughby addressing the group, "for an idea of how the new land could be laid out. If someone could clear that table I'll lay them out on there for everyone to have a decko. Marmaduke drew these up. You see, Marmaduke has been the double agent."

"I thought he was working for Benton?" said Rambo.

"So did Benton," laughed Willoughby. "But he has in fact been working for Harry here all along. He has been the double agent. Harry has outwitted Benton so successfully that it is Benton's money that has given us this means to avoid having to pay Benton's rip-off rent."

Martin threw his head back and roared with laughter, crying, "Very clever! Top work Harry," and reaching across to slap Harry heartily on the back. The group chorused, and added, much praise for a somewhat bewildered Harry.

There was praise also for the hole designs, with the general consensus being that they were much better than the two holes that they were replacing.

"The hole designs will have to be signed off by the Greens Committee," said Rambo haughtily, "the Chairman of the Greens Committee will have to convene a meeting and decide whether to agree them. Everything here has to be done through the appropriate chairman. The proper chairman. Not some voting proxy."

"That's not a problem – Jerry Best has been working with Marmaduke on them," explained Willoughby.

"Everybody apart from me, the Head of the Heads of Committee, seems to have been involved in this," grumbled Rambo.

"Oh no, Rambo, you have been involved in it, too," said the Chairman of Estates. Rambo looked gratified at this acknowledgement. "It's just that the others have actually got something done."

"What is that over there?" asked Wilko, jabbing his finger at a shaded section of the design.

"Oh yes, that area," replied Willoughby, "is earmarked for a putting green. Mrs Winsor has suggested we have one based, as I understand it, on an idea from her daughter Rikki who is studying at St Andrews. Rikki was telling her about the St Andrews Ladies' Punting, er Putting Club, which has a large putting green over which they can lay out a variety of designs for their regular competitions. It apparently is jolly popular with Rikki's housemate Gail."

"Mrs Winsor and Rikki were thinking," Willoughby continued, "that it might be a good idea for Tangents to have one, too, as a way to get people interested in golf and also a way for those that no longer feel up to the slog of tramping up hill and down dale for 18 holes to still meet up with old friends, have some golfing activity, and then retire to the 19th hole for a convivial time and, presuming they are actually allowed to eat food by their other halves, to maybe have some scoff. So Mrs Winsor and Rikki have suggested that the club build one of these also on the land she is leasing to the club. If the club thought this was indeed a good idea, the estate of Godfrey Flower could also pay for its construction. The club could perhaps call it the Godfrey Flower Course."

Anun squeezed Willoughby's arm. "That's a lovely idea. I am sure your friend would have appreciated that."

"Oh, Godders wouldn't have given two hoots," said Willoughby. "He was quite without ego – he was a strange and splendid man like that. But I would like it very much."

"Oh," whispered Anun, "I know Mummy has already told you how delighted she was that you'd fix it so that the club build a halfway hut at Paddock's for her to run, but I would like to thank you, too, in my own way. Everyone is busy looking at the plans, so I'm sure they wouldn't miss us if we nipped out for a while. I want to give you something that I know you do not get at home. There's a handy bush nearby – come on!"

"Is this going to be what I think it is?" said Willoughby, as Anun led him outside by the hand.

"Well, you will just have to wait and see," said Anun teasingly. "Here, if I pull this back you can squeeze through here and it opens up inside. No-one can see us here from the clubhouse." Willoughby realised it was what he thought it was going to be when Anun lifted up her skirt. "Oh what a beautiful sight," Willoughby exclaimed delightedly.

"Ssshh," said Anun, "we don't want anyone to know we're here," as she handed the packet of sandwiches to Willoughby which she had pulled from under her skirt. "Sorry for dragging you in here, but I remember how arsey the Secretary got last time about people eating their own food on the premises."

"Yuff," said Willoughby happily, through an eager mouthful of sandwich.

"Oh hang on. These valuables' pockets are clever at keeping things safely tucked away, but a right pain to get things out of, especially in a decorous manner," said Anun fishing again under her skirt. "That's by way of the pudding course: one of Mummy's macaroons."

"Oh Anun," he said rapturously.

While Anun and Willoughby were hiding away from the Secretary's sight, the Secretary was looking out of his window and saw something that pleased him. It was that the camel had gone. He put this down to his firm leadership and the words he had had with Harry King. Not for the first time, he reflected, if things had to be done round here, it was he, as the Secretary, who was the person to get them done. If only the club was run by him rather than a lot of half-witted committeemen then things would be much better. The Secretary could identify what needed to be done, but then it was left to others to implement the changes – and they didn't.

Take membership numbers: they needed to go up, and they needed to attract younger members. But what was Brian, the membership chairman, doing about it? He had recruited Larry Keane, but as a social member not as a golf member, and he had done it in such a way that the Secretary had no contact information for Mr Keane to check whether this was the wrong category. One good thing about Mr Ramsbotham's food-and-drink card system, the Secretary further reflected, had been that he had been able to work with the Steward to set up an alert whereby when Mr Keane's card was used again, the Secretary could be informed immediately. But the card had only been used that once so far.

The Secretary decided it would be a good idea to go across to the main clubhouse and publicly thank Harry for getting the camel moved. Not that he really deserved much thanks, having taken all this time to do it. But it would be a way of showing to the members how he, as Secretary, was on top of things; that he noticed everything that went on at the club. Never hurts to remind people of this. Also if Brian was there, he could have another attempt at encouraging him to do something to up the membership numbers. The club needed the membership income.

Brian was indeed in the bar. He had just returned and announced that he had seen the camel being removed from the car park.

"Oh excellent, so now we can finally know who had put it there. Who was it? What did they say?" asked someone.

"Who?"

"Whoever it was that was taking it away."

"Oh um I didn't speak to them."

"But didn't you think to ask them, Brian, why it was here in the first place?"

"No need. Harry will know won't he – it's his camel," replied Brian.

Willoughby walked back into the room with both a huge grin on his face and Anun. "Here, you two, have a glass of celebratory Champagne," said Martin proffering two glasses. "You deserve it the most. Top work!"

"That's very kind of you," said Anun. "Thank you."

"Don't thank me. It's come out of the hospitality budget for the Heads of Committee."

"Seems out of character for Rambo?" said Willoughby.

"He's not around at the mo," explained Martin, "don't know where he's got to. So, as temporary acting chairman, I took the decision to order it."

"That'll puzzle him slightly when Champagne appears on his committee inventory, rather than another lot of those ruddy cheese-and-onion crisps," remarked Willoughby.

"He'll be more puzzled than that," laughed Martin. "The receipt is for blue boot polish."

"Do you fancy some of this blue boot polish?" asked Willoughby of Brian, holding out a glass of Champagne which he had taken from the tray.

"Um, no thank you, I um don't have any blue shoes."

"Never mind, have a glass of Champagne, instead," said Willoughby. "Ah, Mr Secretary," Willoughby greeted the newcomer, "come to congratulate Brian? Quite right. Jolly clever of him and the vicar wasn't it?"

"Was it?" said the Secretary "Er, what was?"

"Oh, hadn't you heard? Sorry, I forget how you aren't involved in making decisions here. The club chaplain and Brian have got together and sold some more club memberships. There is going to be a new close built on that scraggy ground on the east of the village, on land partly owned by the church and as joint venture between Miss Gillgrass and Marmaduke, and Brian and our chaplain have negotiated with them that the houses will be sold with 10-year golf memberships as part of the purchase price. So that'll be a nice lot of membership bunce flowing into the club in due course, and hopefully some more bods in here spending money, too."

"You did this Brian?" asked the Secretary. Brian looked at Willoughby, who nodded subtly.

"Yes," said Brian.

"But what has the vicar got to do with it?" demanded the Secretary.

"He is the club chaplain," pointed out Willoughby.

"I know that! But why is he involved?"

"Some of the land was church land, so the padre made the memberships a condition of sale to the developer. Then when Brian heard of that, Brian insisted that the other land also had the same condition applied to that. Shrewd of him, wasn't it, Mr Secretary. I am sure he is too modest to tell you – and I apologise if I embarrass you, Brian – but it took some pretty tough negotiating by Brian to get this agreed, but he succeeded."

"How do you know about the negotiations?" asked the Secretary suspiciously.

"The padre told me. He was very impressed by Brian – sorry again if I embarrass you, Brian."

"Oh I did nothing really", said Brian, moving off. "But thank you, Willoughby."

"So modest," said Willoughby to the Secretary.

"I can't somehow see Brian as a fearsome negotiator," said the Secretary dubiously.

"Can't you? Not fearsome, no, I grant you. But I could see how he could be a tricky man to negotiate with if you didn't know him. He could easily get the other side so utterly confused that they wouldn't be able to follow what's going on. This probably works to his advantage," suggested Willoughby.

"The padre isn't here," he added, "but I am sure you will want to congratulate him too, Mr Secretary, when next you see him. Above and beyond his work as our chaplain, if you ask me, but that's the padre for you. So dedicated to his role at the club."

"There are a lot of people in here," said the Secretary, looking around.

"You still looking for Larry Keane?"

"Why, is he here?" asked the Secretary excitedly.

"Could be – what does he look like?" asked Willoughby.

"I don't know."

"Well that doesn't help much," said Willoughby. "But I'd suggest then why don't you go up to those you don't know and ask them if they are Larry Keane. Men and women: Half Pint pointed out Larry could be a Larissa."

"I'd look a right twit doing that," said the Secretary.

"Sometimes needs must," said Willoughby. "But I suppose the dedication of Brian and the padre is not for everyone."

"Everyone here I seem to know," said the Secretary, relieved. "It appears to be mainly the committee in fact."

"That would probably be because we have just had a committee meeting," said Willoughby.

"Is that what the meeting was about? The sale of these 10-year memberships?"

"No, it was about how we couldn't buy Winnie's Place, so we instead agreed to rent some new land elsewhere, have planned two new holes for it – diagrams over there if you want a decko – and have appointed a new manager of the halfway hut, and are having a practice putting green installed and are hosting a celebration fundraising dinner."

"What! All this decided in one meeting? I knew nothing of any of this!"

"Yes, it was being kept secret. It was on a strictly need-to-know basis I understand."

"But I am the Secretary!"

"Quite," said Willoughby.

They were interrupted by a deliveryman asking them if they'd mind moving over. He was carrying two large boxes of cheese-and-onion crisps.

"Perhaps I oughtn't say this," said Willoughby. "But I believe Rambo said you never make any decisions round here, as you always leave them to the committee chairmen, so Rambo saw no point including you."

"Never make decisions do I," raged the Secretary. He marched up to the deliveryman: "Take those away!"

"And who are you?" challenged the deliveryman.

"I am the Secretary, and I run this golf club and we do not want these crisps. Take them away! Now!"

"I have a docket here, for their delivery," said the deliveryman with the air of one who had just made the clinching argument, holding it out for the Secretary to see.

The Secretary took it, and tore it into pieces. "Now you don't," said the Secretary. "Now take these boxes away!"

"If you say so, but they won't like at base. Won't like it at all. I'm just telling you."

"I couldn't care. Now get out," thundered the Secretary, pointing to the door. "Oh, and Steward, this silly card system. It stops now. Tell them that they have well and truly failed their blasted beta test."

"Excellent decision, Mr Secretary," said Willoughby, "here – have a glass of Champagne."

"Where is Mr Ramsbotham?" said the Secretary looking around. "I need to tell him his card system –"

"His silly card system, you called it," Willoughby reminded him.

"Indeed – his damn silly card system, is over. Where is Mr Ramsbotham? I can't seem to see him."

"No, me neither, and I wanted to give him this receipt for blue boot polish," said Martin coming up.

"Perhaps he was in the camel," said the Chairman of Estates. "Isn't he overdue his afternoon zizz – have you looked in there?"

"The camel has been removed," said the Secretary. "I got Harry to remove it."

"Ah well, never mind," said Willoughby, "I am sure if they find they have got one Rambo that they had not ordered, they will return the goods. Now, can I have everyone's attention for a moment please," Willoughby said loudly, and clapping his hands.

"Has everyone got a glass?" he asked. "Excellent. Then I would like to propose a toast. Partly this is to salute the superb work of our wonderful magician Harry here," a comment which was met with several hearty cries of 'hear hear' – "aided of course by Anun here, in her role as his glamorous assistant, and also to recognise the input of Rikki, with her great insight into golf. Also, of course, we mustn't forget the absent Marmaduke's key role, nor that of the club chaplain and Brian and their clever negotiating skills in flogging those 10-year club memberships to the property developers.

"But most of all, I propose that we all raise our glasses to toast the future of our golf club and my most excellent friend and, more importantly, the club's most excellent friend and benefactor: Godfrey Flower. To Godders!"

"To Godders!" chorused those present.

The End.

By the same author and also published by Brindle Books Ltd

Summer at Tangents

Tangents is a decaying village with a poorly attended church and a struggling golf club. Now the church is threatened with closure. So the vicar's good friend, a wily golf club committee member, acts to save the church in ways which also benefit the club and his friends and involve duping almost everyone along the way.

One of Country Life magazine's Books of The Year for 2024 and nominated for the 2024 Bollinger Everyman Wodehouse Prize for Comic Fiction, Roderick Easdale's hilarious debut novel, Summer At Tangents has received tremendous critical acclaim from a host of publications...

"...a beautifully crafted tale involving many laugh-out loud moments." **(Golf Monthly)**

"Summer at Tangents is a brilliant comic novel but also, ultimately, a feel-good story." **(Golfshake)**

"Roderick Easdale is an authority on P. G. Wodehouse and he is clearly channelling the great author in this rollicking tale of golf-club shenanigans in a very English village. Sentences are brilliantly crafted..." **(Country Life)**

"Author Roderick Easdale effortlessly delivers in this witty, feel-good novel" **(Golf Today)**

"Roderick Easdale, a golf writer of long experience, clearly knows his way around golf clubs and depicts the actions of a cast of colourful and entertaining characters with a real eye for their absurdities, frailties and mostly well-intentioned natures in this witty, warm-hearted, beautifully written, cleverly told story." **(Planet Golf Review).**

9 781915 631268